"We're going to talk like this?"

Nick asked from the rear seat of the limo. "Wouldn't it be more comfortable if we were in the same half of the car?" He stared at the back of Kate's head, but she didn't turn around.

He wondered if he'd be able to explain this to anyone in a way that made sense—the fact that this woman had shown up in his office to ask him out to dinner, had taken him to a restaurant, then changed her mind and was now driving him to who knew where.

He was used to women, but he wasn't used to Kate. And the realization that he hadn't any idea what would happen next caused small ripples of pleasure to travel up and down his spine. His life was filled with excitement. But the feelings stirring in him now were something totally different.

GW00547036

Dear Reader:

Welcome! You hold in your hand a Silhouette
Desire – your ticket to a whole new world of
reading pleasure.

As you might know, we are continuing the *Man of
the Month* concept through to May 1991. In the
upcoming year look for special men created by
some of our most popular authors: Elizabeth
Lowell, Annette Broadrick, Diana Palmer, Nancy
Martin and Ann Major. We're sure you will find
these intrepid males absolutely irresistible!

But Desire is more than the *Man of the Month*.
Each and every book is a wonderful love story in
which the emotional and sensual go hand-in-hand.
A Silhouette Desire can be humorous or serious,
but it will always be satisfying.

For more details please write to:

Jane Nicholls
Silhouette Books
PO Box 236
Thornton Road
Croydon
Surrey
CR9 3RU

SALLY GOLDENBAUM

A FRESH START

Silhouette Desire

Originally Published by Silhouette Books
a division of
Harlequin Enterprises Ltd.

All the characters in this book have no existence outside the imagination of the Author, and have no relation whatsoever to anyone bearing the same name or names. They are not even distantly inspired by any individual known or unknown to the Author, and all the incidents are pure invention.

All rights reserved. The text of this publication or any part thereof may not be reproduced or transmitted in any form or by any means, electronic or mechanical, including photocopying, recording, storage in an information retrieval system, or other-wise, without the written permission of the publisher.

This book is sold subject to the condition that it shall not, by way of trade or otherwise, be lent, resold, hired out or otherwise circulated without the prior consent of the publisher in any form of binding or cover other than that in which it is published and without a similar condition including this condition being imposed on the subsequent purchaser.

First published in Great Britain in 1991 by Silhouette Books, Eton House, 18-24 Paradise Road, Richmond, Surrey TW9 1SR

© Sally Goldenbaum 1990

Silhouette, Silhouette Desire and Colophon are Trade Marks of Harlequin Enterprises B.V.

ISBN 0 373 58132 7

22 – 9104

Made and printed in Great Britain

SALLY GOLDENBAUM

Born in Wisconsin, Sally now lives in Missouri, where she has been successfully writing contemporary romance novels for the past five years, as well as teaching at high school and college levels. Married for almost twenty years, Sally also holds a master's degree in philosophy, and has worked both as a textbook writer and as a public relations writer for public television.

Other Silhouette Books by Sally Goldenbaum

Silhouette Desire

Honeymoon Hotel
Chantilly Lace
Once in Love with Jessie
The Passionate Accountant

One

Nick Bannister pushed his way through the heavy glass doors before the doorman had a chance to move.

He glanced down at the gold watch on his wrist and frowned. Thirteen minutes to get to Pershing and Main. "We're going to have to move it, Jack," he said to the man following closely behind him. "Wiggins hates to wait for anyone."

Jack Stangel nodded and held the door of the limo for him.

"The Amcro Building, Harry," Nick called through the partially opened glass partition that separated him from the chauffeur. "And we're in a hell of a hurry."

Nick dropped his briefcase on the seat opposite him and poured himself a cup of coffee from the small silver pot. The aromatic fumes drifted up and filled the car. "This is the best coffee in Kansas City," Nick murmured. "And it's in a limo. Can you beat that?"

Jack nodded in agreement and reached for a hot croissant. "These aren't bad, either. People don't believe me when I say those extra five pounds came since you hired this limo service. It's God's truth." He leaned forward. "The fact is, Harry knows how to ease the pain of a wild night, right Harry?" Jack grabbed another croissant.

Nick watched the younger man with detachment. Last night had been wild, one more in a whole string of high-powered lengthy business meetings that ended in a party. Nick rubbed the back of his neck with one hand. Damn, he was tired. The nightlife, the parties, the business trips and vacations in Majorca or that little island off Greece—they all filled in hours, kept him moving. Was his body telling him to slow down? Nah. His thirty-six-year-old body wasn't telling him anything, except that maybe he needed a little more sleep. He'd see if he could fit that in.

"What an unbelievable night, Harry," Jack was saying to the driver. "Too much booze, too many women. Is that possible I wonder—too many women? Those California companies know how to make you happy, that's for sure."

Sitting beside the talkative junior executive, Nick wondered briefly about Jack's comment. Again, a wave of unrest swept through him and he took a quick gulp of the hot coffee to block it.

What was he doing analyzing his life? That was best left to the people who got paid for it: his accountants, business managers, financial advisers.

Nick looked out the window at the passing landscape but the pensive mood that had gripped him continued. The limo was speeding past the Country Club Plaza, a beautiful shopping and business area of

Kansas City, and as it nearly always did, the sight brought a smile to his face. Kansas City was beautiful, beautiful enough to block out painful memories. It was peaceful, even quiet on the rare occasions when he wanted that, and was an easy place in which to live. And now it had the added advantage of being half a country away from Elizabeth. That was probably why he stayed, why he hadn't left when his life became disjointed three years ago. He rested his head against the cool headrest and closed his eyes, squeezing away the headache that threatened just behind his lids. Well, sometimes it wasn't so peaceful. Last night, for example.

"Yeah, Harry," Jack went on beside him, a slightly pompous tone in his voice. "Those nighttime business deals will curl your hair. But they're great, just great. Right, Nick?"

"Great?" Nick pulled his eyes open and half smiled. "I don't know if that's the word I'd use, Jack. I use great selectively—for food, good jazz, that sort of thing."

"Come on, Nick, you can't deny those luscious babes don't add a little oomph to your life. We work hard and then we play. All as it should be."

Nick's laugh was short. "Maybe it's for the young, Jack."

"Yeah, right, and those wise words coming from K.C.'s playboy of the year!"

Nick closed his eyes again and continued to talk. "It's all becoming a little predictable in my book. Why is it that some people connect successful business deals with sex? I can almost predict what kind of woman will be at which company bashes. There are the blondes, the full-figures, the bony sort—"

Jack laughed. "But oh, what bones!"

Nick laughed, and then continued. "Sometimes it's tiresome, you know? That kind of parade. Women... hell."

Katherine Alexandra Morelli had had all she could take. Gripping the wheel in her strong, slender fingers, she took the next corner on two tires. The car behind her blasted his horn but Kate didn't notice. Her teeth gritted together and her black brows nearly touched one another above her fiery eyes.

Nick slid sideways on the seat. His words were drowned out by the screech of rubber. Hot coffee sloshed onto his expensive designer suit.

"What the hell are you doing, Harry?" Nick frantically grabbed a stack of linen napkins near the built-in bar and soaked up as much of the liquid as he could. Beside him, Jack swore loudly and swabbed at his burning inner thigh with a white handkerchief.

Kate slammed on the brakes and pushed her chauffeur's cap back on her head. She spun around on the seat, slid the glass partition open wide, and pushed her face through it. "What am I doing? I am taking out my aggressions and hostility on the tires, that is what I am doing!" she shouted, the words bouncing off the limo's padded interior. "And I'm doing that, *sirs*, instead of giving in to the attractive alternative, which is pinning you both to the roof naked and driving to the Amcro building with horns blaring!"

Nick stared at the face that was now just inches from his own.

"And stop staring at me, you fool," she said. "Women *can* do a little more than quench your crude, animal drives you know!" Her green eyes flashed furiously. "Where the cow do you two get off, talking that way?"

"Cow?" The single word slipped from Nick's lips. Where was Harry? And why was this dark-haired woman scolding him?

"Get out," Kate said.

"Out?" Nick glanced out the window. They were on Lindberg Boulevard, stopped in front of a boarded-up old hotel. Small groups of idle teenagers gaped at the shiny, expensive car. Jack let out a hoot of laughter that only infuriated the woman more, and Nick made a mental note to take the fellow off any projects demanding diplomacy.

"Get out of this car," Kate repeated slowly.

Her voice had dropped to a dangerous, low level. It was as smooth and cold as steel. Nick frowned at her. "Hey, lady," he began.

"Kate. My name is not lady, it is Kate. Miss Morelli to you."

"Miss Morelli," Nick said slowly, "my associate, here, and I need to get to a meeting." He checked his watch. "I have five minutes, as a matter of fact, and I presume I am paying a hefty sum of money to this limo company to see that I get there on time. Now I'll let your unorthodox behavior pass, if you'll turn your lovely head around and drive me downtown. Now." The last word was a single shot in the still, charged air.

Kate's blood boiled. She knew she was overreacting, but she'd had it with these hotshot businessmen. Just yesterday she'd taken a call for Billy and had ended up with a five-hundred-dollar offer to make a quick stop in a seedy motel on the way to the airport. And today she was too dog-tired to put it all into perspective. So she'd lose an account. Harry would tell her she was foolish and impulsive, but then, Harry was a man. He didn't understand. She rubbed her eyes, then looked up and found the older of the two men watching her closely in the rearview mirror. She blinked.

"Miss Morelli," he said slowly, "I'm sorry. You're right. We were rude. Now please, will you take us to the Amcro Building?"

Kate continued to stare at him. It was perfectly clear to her that he wasn't the slightest bit sorry. He was angry. Angry with her. But he figured the apology was the only way to get him to his meeting on time.

She considered her alternatives but found they were thin at best. She certainly couldn't remove the men bodily from the car. Her five feet four inches would fit under the boss man's arm. And she didn't want to argue with them anymore. She wanted to get back to the office and have the coffee she'd missed out on when Harry had called in late and asked her to pick up these two irritants. She took a deep breath, flipped the mirror with her fingers to block out the man's piercing blue eyes, then pulled away from the curb with a jerk.

While Nick bit back a curse and soaked up the new spill of coffee from his pants, Kate headed toward Pershing and Main.

"Oh, Harry, don't be such a worrywart." Kate drew her brows together and glared at the short, lumpy man sitting across the table from her in the crowded office.

"Worrywart, my behind. Sometimes, Kate Morelli, you show less sense than God gave a pickle. Nick Bannister's is not an account you can afford to lose, y'know."

"I can afford to lose anyone who threatens my health the way that man did yesterday."

"Health?"

"High blood pressure. That's what you get from chauffering around people like Nick Bannister."

"Nick Bannister," Harry barked, "happens to be the wealthiest man in Kansas City! Worldwide Systems, a company that uses our service enough to support nearly all your unmentionable habits, like eating and keeping warm, Miss Morelli, is not a company to be taken lightly." Harry lit a cigar to calm himself and sat back in the oak captain's chair. It squeaked in protest beneath his weight.

"You didn't tell me who I was picking up," Kate said softly. She was flipping through papers, underlining and making notes as she talked.

"I know, little one, I know," Harry answered with a sigh. "But you would have to be the only person in Kansas City who couldn't recognize him in an instant."

"I wasn't looking at him, Harry. I was looking at the road. Of course I know *of* Nick Bannister. Everyone does. Flamboyant playboys make great gossip. I'm not completely ignorant, you know."

Harry chuckled. Kate was a lot of things, but there wasn't any way on earth she'd ever be able to claim she was ignorant.

"Anyway," Kate was saying, "let's forget about Mr. Bannister for now. He didn't actually say he was cancelling our account. He just got out of the limo and walked away."

Harry rolled his eyes toward the ceiling.

Kate ignored that and waved a sheet of paper. "Now let's move on to other points of interest, Mr. Amatello. Like the Bentley—"

"Kate . . ." Harry pushed himself forward.

"Okay." Kate dropped the sheet on the desk and rubbed the back of her neck. "Okay, okay. I won't buy it today. But when someone grabs it up and we lose out, I'll blame you for the rest of our living days, Harry. You're pussyfooting around like I don't know what, and the car is an absolute steal."

Harry settled back and folded his short, stubby fingers across the bulk of his stomach. "Darlin', that's just one of the reasons I'm against you buying it."

"You think it's hot?"

"Most likely. Sammy Jensen never sold anything clean in his life."

Kate rolled a pencil between her fingers and frowned. That put a different slant on things. The business was going to be perfectly clean and respectable. It held the Morelli name, after all, and Kate was determined not to mar her late-father's reputation. So she surely didn't need stolen cars in her inventory. Harry knew these things. Dear Harry, what would she do without him? Her scowl softened into a smile.

Harry grinned back. "Tell you what, sweetheart, there's a Rolls on auction over at Jake's on the north side. I'm heading that way tomorrow. How about I take a look at it for you?"

Kate's eyes sparkled. "You doll, you. You had that in mind all along."

Harry didn't say anything. Instead he puffed on his cigar while Kate wrote notes willy-nilly on the yellow pad. She knew she could push Harry over with a feather and he'd fall. He'd do anything for her, as long as it was for her own good. He considered it his job.

"I'm not convinced we need a fourth vehicle, kid," he said, "but it's your dough. And we'll get out of it at least what we put in. So it doesn't look like there'll be harm done either way."

"Oh, Harry." Kate looked up. She could feel her cheeks flushing, a tendency she couldn't control no matter how hard she tried. Emotion of any kind—pleasant or otherwise—seemed to ooze directly out of her heart and pores and settle across her cheekbones in a bright wash of color. "What would I do without you, old man?"

"Hell, I don't know." Harry grinned and drew himself up. "Probably get yourself in a heap of trouble. It's those eyes that'll do you in, Kate. They draw all sorts of trouble, quicker than bees to honey. Your pop musta had his head screwed on backwards when he saddled you with this company. You should be—"

"Out in Johnson County with some nice fella having babies. I know, Harry. But it's good of you to remind me since you haven't for a day or two."

"I promised your pop, baby."

Kate rose and soundly kissed his leathery cheek. "I know, Harry, and don't you think for one second I don't appreciate you." It was the plain truth, but appreciation didn't begin to describe what Kate felt for Harry Amatello. It had been less than two years since Kate's parents had been cruelly ripped from her life. A driver, careening down an isolated city street, smashed headlong into Maria and Frank Morelli's small brown car. They had just pulled up in front of their house, having come home late from a family birthday party. Kate guessed they must have felt happy and spirited, filled with the joy of the day, and totally unaware that they would never see another sunrise.

Harry, her father's dearest friend, had been there all through those numbing days, as steadfast as a rock, comforting, consoling, pulling the relatives together in his gruff and kindly way. Much of that time was still a blur in Kate's mind. But the one thing she knew with absolute clarity was that she would never have made it if it hadn't been for Harry.

She watched Harry now as he ambled slowly across the room. He stopped and looked into a small round mirror that hung on one wall. Carefully, with almost a show of reverence, he placed his blue chauffeur's cap on the soft bed of white hair. Then he winked at Kate in the mirror and said in a raspy voice that was filled with laughter, "Oh, Harry, you handsome brute, you."

Kate fondly watched the ritual. Harry was friend, surrogate father, adviser, all wrapped up into one bear-like creature who had never failed her, and what was more, never would. "So, Harry" she said, "looks like you're off."

"Yep, boss. Like a herd of turtles. I've got things to do, people to see—"

"And miles to go before you sleep," Kate finished for him.

"Right-o, Ms. Morelli, ma'am." He tipped his hat and smiled. "I'm taking the White Knight over to that big society meeting off Ward Parkway. Billy finished up with Black Beauty. She's in the garage."

Kate nodded, although she knew exactly where each car had been and would be for the next three weeks. In spite of Harry's worries, they both knew she handled the details of her business with the same care she afforded her plants and Ishmael, the large shaggy dog who had followed her home from Pete's Market one day. He had looked skinny and starved for food and love. Kate had given him both in large doses and he had thrived. And that was what would happen to the Morelli Limo Company. Just a little more love, a little more business.

Kate looked up at Harry. "We really need to get this hospital account, Harry."

Harry reached for a ring of keys from the cabinet near the door. "With your charm, sweetheart, you'll have that hospital hiring us for everything from taking home new mamas and bambinos to tootling their fancy-shmancy board members around town."

Kate walked over to the closet. "Well, I guess we'll soon see. I meet with the head honchos in less than an hour. Do I look all right?"

Harry carefully looked her over, his face a mask of exaggerated concentration. Today she wore a dark green silky blouse and skirt that set off her dark hair. "What a question. Is the Pope Catholic?" Harry said and then he whistled through his cigar-stained teeth.

Kate laughed. "Who needs a magic mirror when there's Harry?"

"Right on, sweetie. You'll wow 'em. Go for it!" He thrust a pudgy fist into the air, then blew her a kiss and walked out, leaving Kate with ten minutes to collect her papers and leave for the Saint Anthony's Hospital monthly board meeting.

Kate sat in a small, tasteful lobby outside the board room. Piped music drifted into the room from some unseen source and a hospital receptionist sat at the single desk knitting a pair of booties. She was pregnant, and Kate wondered absently if she would have the pleasure of driving the woman and her baby home from the hospital in her shiny limo. If they bought the new Rolls, maybe she should have it painted blue and pink and use it solely for hospital trips. No, limiting equipment like that was a bad idea. And a little cheesy, too. But she'd certainly have a pink-and-blue towel wrapped around the champagne bottle inside. And of course there'd be a car seat for the infant that the family could keep. Her mind wandered off to other details and in no time was so lost in thought that she barely heard her name being called.

"Ms. Morelli?" the pregnant receptionist repeated.

"Oh. Oh, yes."

"Well, they're ready for you now." The woman nodded toward the pair of wide doors on the far side of the room. One of the doors was open.

"Ready?" Kate stood. "Ready. Of course. And I'm ready too." She flashed the woman a brilliant smile, pushed her shoulders back to add some height to her frame, and walked confidently into the room.

From his seat at the conference table, Nick Bannister eyed the woman coming in. He noticed the confident lift to her head, the athletic grace to her steps, but most of all he noticed her incredible beauty. It was the kind of beauty that no one made; it simply *was*, like sunsets and soft snow drifts. A simple, breathtaking fact of nature. Nick smiled and indulged himself in the pure pleasure of watching her. Nick loved watching beautiful women.

It wasn't until Kate Morelli began to speak that Nick's smile faded. And it wasn't until she looked him directly in the eye that he realized for certain that he had already met this lovely, calm vision standing at the other end of the table. Except Nick knew that she wasn't really calm at all. Rather, if memory served him right, she was emotional, irrational and feisty as hell.

Two

Kate smiled at the men and women sitting around the table. She recognized Cyrus Hodges from First National. Kate had dealt with him before. He had turned down her first loan, in fact, but she would charm him this time. And there was Sister Maria Frances, director of the board, who introduced Kate. And an accountant she knew by reputation. Kate addressed each person with her eyes, beaming, drawing them in. When her gaze settled on Nick Bannister's somber face, her heart thudded to a standstill. With heroic effort she fought to keep her voice even.

She should have known, should have expected to meet up with him again. But why so soon? Kate's thoughts began to race. No matter what, she absolutely, positively would not let this man's presence botch her presentation; she'd get through it. But how?

Kate briefly looked down on the papers in front of her and took a long, steadying breath.

Her mind cleared. Okay, simple. Piece of cake. She'd do what she always did when she was up against people who sent her blood pressure soaring; she'd pretend he was someone else. But who? A priest, that was it! Yes, a kindly priest who respected professional women and listened objectively to their ideas. A priest was perfect; Kate had always gotten along well with the clergy.

So she met Nick Bannister's eyes and held them confidently as she detailed her proposal to St. Anthony's board in clear, precise terms.

Nick was sure she didn't recognize him. That was clear from her calm expression and the cool way she went about her little speech. But there was no doubt in his mind that she was the same person who had nearly thwarted a million-dollar contract for him by making him late for his meeting. And she owned the damn limo company. Amazing. It was equally amazing that she had any clients left, if she treated them all the way she'd handled him. True, he hadn't cancelled his contract with the Morelli Limo Company, but it was only because of the great coffee and Harry's assurance that he'd be their regular driver from now on. Nick rested his hands behind his head and listened.

By the time Kate was halfway through, Nick had to admit her ideas for the maternity chauffering deal were clever. It was a sound scheme, one that would be good public relations for the hospital. But the fact still remained that Nick had seen Kate Morelli in action, and as good as her plans were, he'd have to explain that she was probably not the best person to do business with.

When Kate called for questions, Nick leaned forward. "Miss Morelli," he said, wanting to see the look of recognition in her face.

There was none.

Nick went on, puzzled. "Miss Morelli, what do you propose to do with the father when he drives over to pay the hospital bill the morning his wife and baby go home? What happens to his car? Or does he drive home alone while his wife is being chauffeured in your fine limo? Surely he deserves some attention, also."

Kate calmly smiled at him. "Of course the new dads deserve special attention. No, they most certainly won't be left out. We've given that careful thought. According to a survey we did, St. Anthony's patients live within a ten-mile radius of the hospital. The chauffeur will pick up the fathers at their homes, have coffee and hot croissants waiting for them—perhaps something stronger if that's their desire or need—" There was a slight ripple of laughter around the table. Kate held her smile and went on. "And then the new family will ride home together in the limo."

She answered him so easily, Nick almost felt foolish for asking the question. And still Kate Morelli showed no recognition. She seemed as calm as a tranquil sea. Amazing.

"Well?" Kate was saying. Her eyes were still on his face, which her imagination had fashioned into that of a kindly, interested prelate. "Does that answer your question, Father?"

The single word slipped out easily. By the time it registered with the board members, a hot, painful flush had begun moving up Kate's neck until it settled uncomfortably across her cheeks and forehead.

"Father?" the accountant repeated, laughter in his voice. He looked over at Nick. "Is there something you haven't told us, Nick?"

"Oh, no," Kate stammered. "Not that kind. A priest..."

Amused sounds rose from the polished oval table.

"I mean," Kate began again, and then she stopped, her heart pounding in her chest. "No," she said simply, looking at him. "Of course you're not a priest."

Nick was smiling slightly. He shook his head. "No, Miss Morelli, I'm not. The religious life has never been my calling, I'm afraid. But you did answer my question."

And she answered all the other questions that followed, somehow putting the moment behind her. A half hour later she thanked the board members for their time and said goodbye. When the door closed behind her, she leaned against it and took a deep, steadying breath. All of Harry's sayings about not burning bridges and covering all bases and exercising prudence and patience came back and bombarded her aching head. She pressed her palms into her temples to block out the sensations.

No, she hadn't burned the bridge. There was still a chance—slight, perhaps, but a chance nevertheless. Most of the others had liked her ideas, she was sure of it. She could tell by the expressions on their faces. Maybe they'd convince Nick Bannister, or vote against him, or—

"Are you all right, miss?" The pregnant receptionist was looking at her strangely.

Kate straightened and smiled at her. She nodded and began walking to the door. "I'm fine, thank you. Yes, I'll be fine. Everything will be fine."

* * *

But when Sister Maria called her late the next day, Kate wasn't really surprised at the news.

"We liked your ideas, Kate. Most of us. It was a clever concept."

"But..."

"But I feel it's only fair to tell you that Cyrus Hodges has some reservations."

"And..."

"Well, Mr. Bannister feels it might not be to the hospital's benefit to sign a contract with you just now."

"Why?"

"Well..." Sister Maria paused.

"It's all right, Sister. Tell me."

"He seem to think, well, that you are not the kind of business person we want to deal with. Now I disagree with him, and I told him so in no uncertain terms. But he seems to have some definite feelings against your management abilities, Kate."

"I see."

"We won't decide until we have a chance to talk again. We'll meet next week, but I thought it was only right that I call and tell you where things stand now."

"I appreciate that, Sister." Kate doodled fiercely on the pad beside the phone. Then a note of hope crept into her mind. "Well, no matter, Nick Bannister is only one person, right?"

Sister Maria gave a soft laugh. "No, Kate," she said. "Nick Bannister is not a single person. Nick Bannister is a whole dynasty."

Kate sighed, hung up the phone and reached for a doughnut.

Harry found her still sitting there an hour later.

"Hey, there were four doughnuts in that bag when I left. There're none left. What did you do, Morelli, have a party?"

Kate wiped a crumb from the corner of her mouth. "Not exactly." Then she recounted her conversation with Sister Maria.

"Don't let it get you down, Morelli. Because there's work to be done today. You are now the proud owner of one shiny red Rolls. So get off that lovely duff and convince St. Tony's they need us."

"Harry!" Kate jumped up and threw her arms around him. "You did it! You got the car."

"You doubted me?" Harry said.

"How did you pay for it?"

"We'll worry about the details later."

"You're wonderful, Harry. And how can I let a little thing like Nick Bannister get me down? I won't, that's all!"

"Spoken like a true Morelli. There's more than one way to skin a cat, y'know."

"You're darn right."

"Never give up the ship."

"Right, Harry."

"Rome wasn't built in a day, you know."

"Harry, stop!" Laughing Kate dropped the last of her doughnut on the desk. At the same time, an idea began to blossom in her brain. She wiped off her hands on a tissue, slipped into her coat and headed for the door.

Harry didn't question her quick exit. "May the wind be at your back, my darlin'," he called across the room.

"That's Irish, Harry," she tossed back over her shoulder.

"It's called covering all your bases. Now be off and be happy."

Harry lowered his bulk into the swivel chair behind the desk. "Ciao," he said softly as the door slammed shut behind her.

Kate had never been inside the Bannister Building, even though it was a Kansas City landmark and the site of many civic galas and charity functions each year. She looked around the huge black-marble lobby and thought about her own tiny office over on Southwest Trafficway. It would easily fit into the space allotted the information desk and security office behind it, she thought. But that wouldn't deter her. Big meant nothing. Nick Bannister, for all his marble lobbies and money, was simply a person, like anyone else. He simply needed a little more convincing. And Kate would provide that free of charge. She walked over to the bank of shiny elevators and carefully read the directory. Executive offices sixteenth floor.

Involuntarily, Kate looked up.

All right, sixteenth floor it would be. She stepped back into the waiting elevator and without giving herself the chance to change her mind, she pressed her finger against the round button. Tightly closing her eyes, she wished for luck as she was whisked up to Worldwide Systems' executive suites.

Nick stood in front of the curved expanse of windows in his office and looked down on the fountains below. The water would be shut off soon, he thought. But even in winter there was a beauty to the pools and statues that were spread out across the Plaza. The stone statues would stand tall and majestic as they collected snow on their smooth shoulders and arms, the pools would become soft white beds. He looked out across the Spanish-style buildings of the shopping area to the western horizon. From his spot, he could see all the way into Johnson County and its sleeper communities, which not so many years ago had been farms and woods and fields of waving golden wheat. The sun was setting now, beyond the highways, and people were rushing home for their evening meal with their families. It was a good city, in spite of everything. It was his city.

Nick turned back to the desk, appreciating his good fortune in having five minutes without the plant phone ringing or Sylvia buzzing him about the latest emergency. "Thank God for small favors," he murmured aloud, just before a noisy commotion broke out in Sylvia's office.

"But I must see him!" the unseen person said.

The voice was insistent, and louder than most voices in the tasteful, muted suite of offices. He frowned and then listened as the voice rose even louder. The person obviously didn't know Sylvia, his secretary, he thought with detachment. Behind her placid face and rather dowdy middle-aged form, was a Herculean strength that protected Nick almost to a fault.

At that moment, the heavy door swung open and shattered his last thought.

Kate Morelli stood in the doorway, her dark hair still moving from her hurried entrance. Flecks of gold danced in her flashing eyes and a wash of pink coloring highlighted her cheekbones.

Nick stared at her.

"I'm sorry, Mr. Bannister!" Sylvia's shrill voice came flying over Kate's shoulder. She was incensed at the impudence of the stranger; Nick could see it in the angry lines of her face. "She simply barged right in!" Sylvia said.

"I need to see you," was all Kate said.

Her voice was steady but it had a rich, husky undertone that made Nick clear his throat involuntarily. "That's all right, Sylvia," he said at last. "I'll see Miss Morelli for a few minutes."

"Thank you." Kate's solemn expression melted into a broad smile. "Thank you very much. I don't need much time—"

Sylvia's stern cough expressed her objections, but she dutifully left Kate alone with Nick, closing the door behind her. He stood across the room looking at her.

"I felt you needed some more information," Kate began.

"About the St. Anthony's proposal?"

"Yes."

"Sit down, then."

Kate gratefully sank into an upholstered chair on one side of Nick's wide desk while he sat down behind it. Her legs were shaking so badly she knew she would have sunk down to the floor if he hadn't suggested she sit. The solid chair revived her considerably and she plunged right in. "I don't think you've looked at my company closely enough to—"

The ring of the red telephone in the middle of Nick's desk cut off her sentence. Kate stared at it. It looked like the president's private phone that she had seen in movies.

Nick talked into the mouthpiece for a minute, then hung up and directed his attention back to Kate. "You were saying about your company."

"I was saying that you need to judge it on its merits—" Again the red phone intruded rudely.

Nick automatically reached for it, spoke calmly in the same low tones, then hung up. "That's my plant phone," he explained. "The employees there know they can always reach me. Now, you were saying?"

"I was saying that you shouldn't make hasty decisions without—"

"Decisions?"

The door opened and Sylvia walked in with a letter in her hand. "I'm sorry, Mr. Bannister, but this was delivered by the Amcro messenger with directions that you were to get it immediately."

Nick opened the envelope and read the message carefully while Sylvia stood waiting. Kate thought that she was probably as dedicated as she was competent. She didn't look at Kate but gave Nick her absolute attention. When he finally looked up, he spoke a few words to Sylvia, she took a few notes and she was gone.

"Efficient," Kate said. Hope was shrinking into a tiny ball in her chest. It was clear she wasn't up to this competition—the red phone *and* Sylvia.

"Extremely," Nick said. "Now, about your concerns."

Kate stood up abruptly. "Would you like to have dinner with me?" She glanced at her watch. "It's almost that time, and surely you eat."

Nick looked at her. "Dinner?"

"Yes. Now. We can walk over to the Plaza."

Nick frowned. And then the frown gave way to a smile, as he thought of the ludicrousness of the situation. He had dinner invitations he hadn't begun to read stacked on a table in his front hall at home. Cov-

eted invitations. And here was this stranger, this wisp
of a thing inviting him—on five minutes' notice.

"Don't worry," Kate said heading for the doorway. "I'll treat."

"Well, in that case how can I refuse?"

"You can't." Kate laughed, and with a toss of her
head she walked past a puzzled Sylvia and into the
thickly carpeted hallway. Nick followed close behind.

When Kate and Nick entered Starker's restaurant in
the Country Club Plaza, they were led immediately to
a choice spot near the windows. Several diners greeted
Nick as they passed between the linen-covered tables.
Twice they stopped while Nick dutifully cheek-kissed
glamorous women who rose from their chairs like he-
lium balloons. Kate chose to ignore the glances that
were then given her. Obviously she wasn't Nick's usual
kind of companion.

"They know you here," Kate said as they sat down.
"I should have thought of that."

"Kansas City is a small town in many ways."

Kate nodded and accepted the champagne cocktail
that miraculously arrived for her. Nick sipped his dry
martini thoughtfully. "I think that's why I like it here.
It's small and large, whichever way you want it."

A man in an elegant pin-striped suit appeared before them, smiling briefly at Kate as Nick made intro-
ductions. He then proceeded to engage Nick in a short,
charged discussion of a motion before the city council to build a high rise east of the Plaza. Kate noticed
that Nick's opinion seemed to be very important to the
other man.

When he left, Nick shrugged. "A lot of business is done over Starker's great food," he explained. "I guess I'm fair game here."

Kate nodded. While he was talking she noticed several other people looking at him. Planning their attack, she guessed. Coming to Starker's had been her idea and apparently a bad one. Kate's mind mulled over other possibilities. She had made two strikes already. Only one chance left.

"Do you mind if we leave?" Kate stood suddenly and dropped her napkin beside her plate.

"Leave?" Nick scowled and stared hard at Kate. But his scowl immediately changed to a look of concern. "Are you sick?"

"No. Well, maybe I am, I don't know. I might be." She *would* be, if she didn't get his attention for ten minutes without the whole world stepping in and making itself heard! Kate took small, sliding steps toward the door while she talked.

Nick continued to examine her. On second thought, she didn't really look sick. The flush on her cheeks was a healthy one. Healthy and sexy, now that he'd had a chance to think about it. In fact, she looked beautiful. Her eyes were shining and the room's candlelight cast a soft glow around her, tempting Nick to reach out and touch her to see if she was real.

"I know that you're hungry," Kate said, still moving away from the table.

"That's right. And this is a terrific restaurant. And if you're trying to convince me you run a stable, efficient company, this isn't exactly the way to go about it." He had gotten up and was following her now, his drink still in his hand.

Kate frowned. That was certainly true. But she couldn't hold his attention in here. It wasn't much better than the office. She paused at the leaded-glass entrance doors and half turned toward him. "I know. You must think me scatterbrained, but I'm not. All I want is a little of your time, but I need your complete attention. I can't get that here."

"But dinner—" Nick glanced back toward the table.

"We'll get food. Trust me."

Nick glanced over to the maître d' and held up his martini glass. "I'll bring this back later, Jack. Sorry." He shrugged, half smiled and followed Kate out onto the street. He wondered briefly if he'd fallen out of bed during the night and somehow failed to remember the blow to his head. He sure as hell couldn't figure out why he was following this unpredictable woman around instead of sitting down to a second martini and a Starker's K.C. strip.

"Here," Kate said a few minutes later. "Get in." They had walked back toward the Bannister Building and were now standing beside a shiny, stretch limo that was parked at the curb.

"Is this yours?"

"No, Nick, I just saw it here and decided, what the heck, let's go for it." Her voice leveled off. No need to get feisty. Wasn't that what had gotten her into big trouble with this man in the first place? "Yes," she said softly. "It's mine. The Morelli Limo Company's, at any rate, and Commerce Bank's. This is the White Knight."

"How do you do?" Nick said solemnly.

Kate laughed and opened the door.

"She's a beauty, Kate." The car was spotless and rubbed to such a high sheen that he could see himself in the doors. "I don't think I've met this one."

"No. We use Black Beauty for most of our executive runs." She motioned for Nick to get in the back seat. As soon as he had, she walked around the long, elegant hood, opened the driver's door and slipped behind the wheel.

"We're going to talk like this?" Nick asked through the open partition. "Wouldn't it be more convenient if we sat in the same half of the car?" Nick wondered if he'd be able to explain this to anyone in a way that made sense—the fact that this woman had shown up in his office, taken him to dinner, untaken him to dinner, and now was taking him to God only knew where. It didn't make any sense to him, except for one thing. No one, at least now within recent memory, had intrigued him quite the way Kate Morelli did.

"We'll talk in a minute," Kate was saying. She turned a corner, then pulled into an alley between two blocks of elegant stores. She stopped at a sign that said GOURMET GROCER: Drive-in window. In the space of five minutes, Kate had given an order and then received two bulging bags from a smiling white-aproned man. The limo was immediately filled with a tantalizing assortment of delicious aromas, but before Nick could ask any specifics, Kate was maneuvering the car out of the alley and toward the wide stretch of Ward Parkway that would take her away from the Plaza.

Nick put his head back against the plush seats and sipped his martini. He smiled. He was used to limos. He was used to women in all shapes and sizes. But he wasn't used to Kate Morelli. And the realization that he hadn't any idea what would happen next was causing small ripples of pleasure to travel up and down his spine. His life was filled with excitement—big-time business excitement that manipulated millions of dollars and affected nearly as many lives. But the feelings stirring in him now in the dark shadows were a totally different breed. Kate Morelli, for all her unorthodox ways, was arousing Nick and the feeling was too good to ignore. He closed his eyes. When the car stopped a few minutes later, he was still smiling.

Before he had time to register much of anything, Kate was in the backseat, opposite him, making herself comfortable.

Nick peered through the windows. "The rose garden?" he said curiously.

Kate grinned. "Yes, a lovely place to dine, don't you think?" They were in the parking lot of Loose Park, facing the stone entranceway to the gardens. The small duck pond was just visible, off to the side. While Nick became adjusted to where he was, Kate busied herself setting the teak car table with elegant, hand-painted plates. She took a bottle of wine from the built-in cabinet and filled two crystal glasses. Soft music filtered through the car and tiny lights on the upholstered sides sent shadows dancing across the soft leather.

"Amazing," Nick murmured as he watched Kate go to work on the white grocery bags. Carefully, she spooned a plump chicken breast smothered in some rich, fragrant wine sauce onto each plate. Crisp broccoli spears and artichoke salad followed. "There," she said at last. Kate lifted her glass to Nick's and smiled over its rim. "Here's to quiet business dinners."

Nick shook his head. Then he lifted his glass and smiled warmly. "And to an extraordinary hostess."

Kate nodded, accepting the compliment. She felt a mood wrapping around them that hadn't been included in her hastily put-together plans. When she looked over at Nick, she strongly suspected he felt it, too.

Nick sipped his wine. It was a good zinfandel. The music was tasteful, too, a quiet, moody Mozart violin concerto. He wondered if Kate knew what kind of a mood she was dishing up here. He thought not, but then, what did he know about Kate Morelli? Maybe he had her pegged all wrong and she was a far different kind of business woman than he suspected. He shoved the thought aside almost as soon as it materialized. No, that didn't fit. And it went against the pleasure that continued to course lazily through his body. She wanted him to be comfortable, that was all, so he would listen to her.

Kate waited until Nick had taken a large bit of chicken before starting in. "Nick, I want to talk to you about the Morelli Company's proposal to Saint Anthony's."

The chicken was fantastic. A great, sensual way to spend a couple of hours, he thought. He'd been entertained in more ways than he could remember, but this was a first. Nick took another drink of wine.

"The proposal," Kate said again. He hadn't seemed to hear her. Maybe she should have ordered something less tasty, a plain turkey sandwich or ham on rye. Nick seemed entranced by the food.

Nick looked over at her. "Oh, sure," he said reluctantly. "The proposal. It was a good presentation." He eyed Kate's chicken.

She forked it over to his plate. She was starving, but it was all for a good cause. "I want you to know a few more facts before the board makes its decision.'' Kate took a quick sip of wine and then plunged in, not giving Nick a chance to speak. She detailed the brief history of her ownership of the company, explained to Nick how it was actually given to her father in exchange for some long-time debts just before he died. And then it passed on to her. She didn't explain that it was *all* that went to her; that when the estate was settled, the battered limo company was all that was left, her dubious legacy. So she had given it her parents' name and promised at their grave that she would make it good, make them proud of her.

She finished her explanation with a list of contracts she already held and a mention of her spotless accident record. She told him how she'd extended the fleet of limousines, how she had three full-time drivers. When he had finished the chicken and was eyeing the chocolate cream pie, she told him how her profits were up and then dished him up a huge helping. During coffee she explained that it would make the bank very happy if she had a few more firm contracts under her belt, like the Saint Anthony's service to new parents, for example.

"I see," Nick said. He accepted the snifter of brandy that she held out to him

"Do you?" Kate was watching him intently, trying to read his face. He was more relaxed, so she knew he was enjoying himself. But was he listening?

"Yes, I do," Nick said.

Kate felt a little easier. "Well, good. All I ask is that you think about what I've told you."

In the soft, hazy light, her beauty seemed to take on new dimensions, Nick thought. It was even more arresting than in the brighter glare of his office. Thick lashes had brushed her cheeks while she talked and her breasts rose and fell with the momentum of what she was saying. She was probably totally unaware of the impact she was having on him. Nick shifted on the seat. Talk, say something, he prompted himself. Cool the air here. "Kate," he said out loud, "tell me something about you, what you did before you got into the limo business."

Kate hesitated. She didn't want to talk about herself, especially right now with her hormones doing high jumps and with Nick's knee a fraction of an inch from her own. But maybe her past was relevant and he had a right to ask her a few questions. She'd keep her answer simple, direct. "I did a lot of things. The most recent job before this was running a nanny service. Before that I hung around Europe for a while. I was an au pair in Paris and took some painting classes. I was kind of a museum groupie, I guess." She laughed self-consciously. She moved while she was talking and her knee lightly touched Nick's. She could feel the slight pressure travel upward along every nerve ending in her body. "And I worked at Swanson's department store for a few months," she added quickly, anxious to think about neutral, everyday, humdrum things.

"Did you like it?" It was an idiotic question, but Nick was so distracted by her nearness that his thoughts were becoming cloudy and disconnected.

"Like it?" Kate met his question seriously. "Well, I miss the discount." And then she laughed softly, a throaty sound that made Nick take another sip of brandy.

"You said you took painting classes," he said. "Are you an artist, too?"

Kate shrugged. She wasn't sure what *else* he thought she was. "I was an art-history major in college. But I never finished school."

"Why?"

His eyes were watching her so carefully. Kate looked down, then slowly lifted her head and began to talk again. "Oh, a lot of reasons. Money for one. There wasn't any. But even if there had been, I might have quit. I like to learn things hands-on. It made more sense to me to read the books and then travel around and see it all. I'd sit in front of the paintings and they told me what they were all about, you know? It was far more real than the books." She was animated now and leaned forward.

Nick nodded. "It makes sense, sure." His voice was strained. He was listening closely and found everything that spilled out of her mouth interesting. He wanted to hear more. He wanted to know what Kate thought, and why she thought the way she did. He wanted to know if she had a man in her life— A sharp stab of desire nearly lifted him from the seat. Nick shifted toward the window. He rested one hand against the glass and tried to pull the coolness into his body through his skin. He looked back at Kate.

"You're anxious to go," she said quickly, deliberately misinterpreting his movement. She'd felt it, too: the sudden charged tension in the air; the pull that caused her breath to catch in her throat. It jarred Kate, forced her to shake her head slightly to stabilize her emotions. No, this wasn't what she had intended; this was *not* what the evening was all about. This could ruin everything. She took a breath and smiled brightly at Nick. "I know I've taken up too much of your time."

Nick pulled himself forward on the seat. Movement was good; it cleared his head a little and forced some sanity back into his fuzzy brain. "Well, it was worth it. The meal was great. The setting, the whole works."

"Well, good. The Morelli Limo Company aims to please."

"And it succeeds." Small talk, chatter. Nick hated it. But it was working, pulling some focus into the night.

Kate stashed the dishes in a plastic-lined hamper and wiped the table. She tossed the cloth in a bag. "I'll have you back in no time. Just let me get back into the driver's seat." Yes, that was what she needed, to get back in the driver's seat. Keep this thing in perspective. Good grief, she had almost attacked the man. Every nerve in her body had screamed at her and demanded contact. But she'd controlled it, thank God. She was trying to convince Nick Bannister she was competent, not a nymphomaniac!

Nick drank a glass of ice water in one long swallow and drew his body into the most uncomfortable position he could find. There, he'd done it, quieted the savage beast. He brought his face up to the glass partition. "Thanks, Kate," he said at last.

"Oh, sure." Kate gunned the engine. "Now where to, the office building?" She pulled the car onto Wornall, turning left.

"Fine," Nick answered. He sat back, as far away from her as possible, and glanced at his watch. They'd been together for four hours. Nick couldn't decide if it seemed like seconds, or a lifetime.

"Here you are," Kate said a few minutes later. Her voice was pleasant but businesslike. She smiled at him. "Thanks again for your time."

"It was well spent," Nick murmured as he slid out of the car. He stood for a minute at her window while she rolled it down, and then he bent over. He was careful not to get too close. The fires weren't completely dampened. "'Night, Kate."

"Good night, Nick. I hope you'll mull over Morelli Limo. We're a good company."

Nick nodded. A wind picked up some leaves and blew them around his legs, but all he felt was the warmth from the car. "Sure," he said. He tapped the roof lightly with two fingers. "I'll do that." He took one more look at Kate, then turned and walked slowly toward the bright night lights guarding his building.

Kate sat still for a minute and watched him. His head was bare and the breeze carelessly tossed his thick sandy hair. He didn't seem to notice. He was an unusual man, she thought. He'd impressed her, angered her, excited her, all in such a short space of time. There was a mystery about him, something behind the much-publicized figure of the president of Worldwide Systems. Maybe that was what had gotten to her, the suspicion that there was far more to Nick Bannister than money and women and marble lobbies.

She sighed and rolled up the window. Too bad, she thought. She pulled the limo away from the curb and merged with the evening traffic on Main Street. It was too bad Nick wasn't just a nice guy she'd met at a party, a normal guy she could talk to and be with.

Someone she'd feel free to get to know a lot better. Too bad, because the feelings that were finally quieting down inside of her told her she'd sure like to get to know Nick Bannister a whole lot better.

Three

——

Tuesday it rained.

Kate stood in her robe and worn slippers and stared out at the cold, gray day. Behind her on the linoleum floor sat a large aluminum pot that announced each drop of water with a lonely, hollow sound. Kate barely heard the noise. Her mind was crammed full of thoughts that had nothing to do with the weather or the condition of her roof.

And Nick Bannister was responsible for it all—for the anger, the confusion, and even the feelings she chose not to give credence to. They were all his fault, the whole kit and caboodle. He'd gone and used his almighty influence to convince the board that the Morelli Limo Company wasn't a good bet. She had made a perfect chump out of herself the other night. And she had actually thought that she and Nick Bannister had connected on some level.

Kate bit her bottom lip. At first she had seethed when Sister Maria had called and told her the outcome of the meeting. She had been so mad at what must have been Nick's influence in the whole thing that she hadn't even asked Sister for any details. Rubbing salt in the wound wasn't Kate's style. But the anger soon gave way to other more complicated emotions.

Kate was confused. She prided herself on reading people accurately, but she'd sure missed on this one. She had thought she'd seen something in Nick beyond the society pages' presentation. She thought there was real depth there that went beyond the handsome, womanizing playboy she'd heard about. But she was wrong. Nick Bannister was not the person she had imagined him to be. Behind the attentive facade and that sexy half smile, he had probably been laughing at her all night, just as Gregory Hutton had done all those years ago. Men—especially rich ones—were the pits, a lesson she should have learned a long time ago.

The telephone rang, but Kate ignored it. The insistent buzzing gnawed away at her nerves until she was finally forced to lift the receiver.

The wheezing at the other end of the line told her it was Harry.

"Hello, Harry."

"Okay, dumplin'," he said. "When do you hit up St. Joseph's?"

"Harry, why are all these hospitals named after saints? There's nothing remotely saintly about the way they're treating me!"

"Hey, is that self-pity I hear? Morellis don't know about self-pity, kid."

"You're right, Harry. I go to St. Joe's today."

"And they'll buy the idea hook, line and sinker. You mark my words, doll."

"Okay, Harry."

"Now why the sound of a funeral in your voice, Katherine?"

"I was wrong about Nick Bannister, Harry. And I think I made a fool of myself."

"That, my bambina, happens to all of us now and again. Even to yours truly, believe it or not. Put it aside, kiddo, and move ahead. It's another day, another dollar."

Kate began to answer, but Harry had hung up. He didn't like telephones and never said goodbye. It made the retreat faster, Kate supposed, but she had never gotten used to it. Yet maybe Harry had the right idea; maybe there was something to hasty retreats. She tossed aside the gloom of the weather and Nick Bannister and headed for the shower. Harry was right about one thing, for sure. It was another day and if she didn't get her act together soon, there might not be another dollar.

Kate dressed carefully for her second appointment with a hospital board of directors in less than a week. She'd be glad when this was over with and she could go about her business of running limos. Besides, she was running out of business suits, not that that was so astounding. When you had two, going through them didn't take a long time.

She straightened the collar of her soft cream-colored blouse and glanced briefly in the mirror on her closet door. There. She hoped she had hit the right combination today: part businesswoman with the deep green suit, part convent schoolgirl, and just a small dash of frill. Maybe that was what bothered Nick Bannister the other day: no frill. Well, whatever it was, it didn't matter. Nick Bannister was past history. And that brief spark of attraction she'd felt was probably nothing more than hunger. Or a touch of the flu. The man was a Benedict Arnold, not romantic material, at all. He was about as far removed from the kind of man she'd be interested in as the king of Siam.

Kate vigorously brushed her hair as she put her thoughts in order. With quick, nimble movements she arranged the thick tresses into a French braid that began at the top of her head and hung down thick and shiny between her shoulder blades. A touch of lipstick and she felt ready. She glanced at her watch. It was two o'clock. No time to eat. Served her right for frittering away the day with unproductive thoughts. She collected her briefcase, pressed a hand to her stomach to calm the butterflies, and headed for the door. There was no use postponing the inevitable. Time to go.

Two hours later Kate walked down the gray hospital steps into a pool of bright, blinding sunshine. The rain was gone and she threw her head back and grinned up into the clear sky. "We did it, Pop!" she said out loud. "They loved it!"

The only answer was the growl of her stomach.

The board members had loved every idea that slipped from her lips. And this board didn't even need a few days to discuss it; the members all agreed right then and there that hers was a unique idea. Although they'd need some time to hash out the details, the proposal was a winner and provided a service they'd definitely offer to their parents if the terms were right. And the terms would be— Kate would see to that.

She was sorely tempted to call Nick Bannister and tell him how wrong he had been, and that because of him St. Anthony's was losing out and another hospital would be the first to offer its new parents a ride home from the hospital in style.

But a second growl from inside of her blurred the thought, and instead, she drove directly to Marco Polo's Deli where she ordered two gigantic bratwurst, each one drenched in thick brown mustard and sandwiched into a crisp, hard roll. She restrained herself from eating just long enough to drive to the park, find a parking place, and slide out of the car. The park smelled fresh, washed clean by the morning rain. It was the perfect accompaniment to her first meal of the day.

Kate walked slowly along the edge of a small pond and savored the taste of the spicy pork sausage. The smell of moist earth filled her nostrils and she held her shoulders back, letting the day freely assault her senses. Running the limo business these past months had been a real roller-coaster ride, and it was nice at last to be on the up track.

She wiped a crumb from the corner of her mouth and headed up a small rise of land. The ground was muddy and she concentrated on her footing as bare stretches of ground slid beneath her. In a little over an hour, Kate felt replenished in every way—her spirit lifted, her hunger assuaged, her physical self and self-esteem revitalized. Tossing the wax sandwich wrapper into a round refuse can, she smiled into the crisp breeze and decided to treat herself to one more circle of the park before darkness descended completely. And then she'd go home, call Harry with her wonderful news, and maybe splurge on a movie. She certainly deserved it.

So intent was Kate on the evening ahead that she didn't see the tuxedoed figure until she was nearly at the edge of the park. He was walking alone on a narrow pathway that wound between the trees and across the green fields. The hazy glow of twilight outlined him, setting his tall, imposing figure apart from everything else in her line of vision. He was a black-and-white knight, an anachronism here in the lush, green park with its touring bikes and carefully groomed dogs on leashes.

Kate's breathing stopped at the same time her feet did. At first she thought her mind was playing tricks on her. But the man's assured movements jarred her senses and she saw that this was no trick. The knight was really Nick Bannister and that realization propelled Kate over to a clump of trees both to avoid the man who had nearly ruined her day, and to get a better look.

But her high heels and suit did her in. She simply didn't function well in either. As she sailed around the tree, one heel caught on a raised root, and before she could register fear or dismay, Kate's feet had flown out from beneath her and she was tumbling down a short, rain-slick knoll.

Nick heard the quick, sliding sound of a body tumbling and then a short series of low-pitched expletives. He headed toward the noise without a thought, and in a few long strides he was at her side. She was trying to get up, her elbow pushed into a muddy hollow and her back facing him.

"Can I help you, miss?" he asked.

Kate didn't answer. Instead, she shuddered, then slowly turned her sore body toward him.

"Well, I'll be damned," he muttered, a frown pulling his brows together.

Nick was staring down at her with such intensity that Kate wondered briefly if the mud had somehow dissolved her clothes right off her body. On second thought, it wasn't that kind of a look. No, maybe she had grown two heads.

"Yes," was all she said.

"Are you okay?" Nick finally asked, concern belatedly showing in his voice.

"Of course not. But I'll live, thank you."

"I'm sure of that."

Kate continued her efforts to rise, but she slipped again in the soil. She could feel a tear in her skirt and the shreds of her stockings were clinging to her wet ankles, but she ignored them and tried to force a calm expression onto her face.

"Here, let me help you." Nick bent over at last and placed his hand firmly beneath her elbow. His fingers wrapped around her sleeve and he lifted her easily to her feet. Kate started to slip again and grabbed his arm. A quick glance at Nick's black tuxedo made her let go. Everything she touched turned to mud. "Sorry," she murmured. And then she added, "That's interesting dress for a stroll in the park."

"I was on my way somewhere."

"Oh."

"Over there." He pointed to a large home that faced the park. Kate could see a line of cars dropping off elegantly dressed couples in the circular drive. "Are you sure you're all right?"

"Yes. But you're going to stand out in that crowd looking like that."

Nick glanced at his clothes. He shrugged. "It'll come off. But—" his eyes scanned her body "—you're . . . you're a mess."

"Thank you," she said, tightening her lips.

"I'm sorry, I only meant—"

"No. You're right, I am a mess." She looked down at her suit and thought of the expense a joyful walk had caused her. An hour ago her day was nearly perfect. Somewhere between then and now she'd taken a wrong turn. She poked at a flattened pancake of mud on the pocket of her jacket.

Nick watched her and was struck again by her beauty. He'd thought of her often the past few days. He didn't know what it was about her, maybe her brazenness or her innocence, or maybe the contrast between the two, but she made him want to smile in a way he hadn't smiled for a long time. And even now, with her splattered clothes and face, he marveled at how lovely she looked. Showing through it all was that intriguing glow. "This breeze is cold," he said finally. "You should get inside."

Kate nodded.

Nick was puzzled. She seemed so nonchalant about the whole thing. He thought he understood a lot about women, and in this situation, most of the ones he knew would have slid behind a bush or rushed off to some salon to have the damage repaired. Kate seemed only vaguely aware of her dishevelment, and what awareness she had was only of a practical nature. He watched her as she rubbed her fingers together. Muddy flakes fell to the ground.

"Do you want to come home with me?" he asked.

Kate felt tiny hairs rise on the back of her neck. "Home with you . . ." She held her head back to look him directly in the eyes, forced a smile onto her face and spoke as sweetly and calmly as she could. "Are you crazy, Bannister?"

Nick was wondering the same thing and her retort made him smile back, which seemed to infuriate Kate even more.

She poked a finger into his chest. "You, Nick Bannister, are one arrogant . . . person!" Her eyes blazed. "First you nearly ruin my business, then you try to prey on my defenseless situation here and make a suggestion like . . . like that!"

"Hey." Nick held out both hands to fend off her anger. He had no idea what she was talking about concerning her business, but he'd have to deal with that later. "I didn't mean what you're thinking. All I meant was you need to clean yourself off."

"Believe it or not, I have running water at my house, too."

"But I live right there." He pointed across the park.

Kate lifted her brows, her anger forgotten for a second.

"You can clean up there, then be on your way."

Kate started to argue, then stopped. She'd ruined her suit and shoes; there was no sense of ruining her car, as well. If she could just scrape off enough of this to save the seat cushions, she'd avoid that cleaning bill, at least. "What about your party?" she asked cautiously.

"It'll wait." He took her elbow and began walking briskly.

Kate started to resist. She hadn't forgotten the large bone that was still there between them, waiting to be picked. But a cold breeze made her shiver and she decided there was a time and place for everything and this was not the time to pick the bone. Besides, she rationalized as she struggled to keep up with his long, loose strides, he was being sort of decent and who was she to deny him his moment of good citizenship? It might be the last one he would ever have.

The house he led her to was right across the street from the park, in a neighborhood of huge, elegant homes. But this one was set so far back from the street that Kate had never noticed it before. "You live here?" Kate said softly. It wasn't really a question, but rather words to cover up the awe she felt as they walked down the wide brick walkway. Suddenly Kate was acutely aware of every bit of mud, of every twig, that clung to her body. "Oh, I can't—" she started.

"It's all right," Nick said. He looked down at her and offered a slow smile. "We won't be alone. There's a man who helps me, and a cook."

"I didn't mean that," Kate snapped. "I'm not afraid to be alone with you, Mr. Bannister. I was referring to my state."

Nick looked her over. Kate felt the power of his gaze and her limbs began to feel weak. She'd experienced the same sort of thing in the limo the other night, but somehow, with Nick standing there looking so elegant, the effect was far more forceful. Kate found herself unnerved and uncomfortable. "I'm going to go home," she said.

"If it's the dirt you're worried about, I think it's just fine—as dirt goes, that is."

Now he was being coy. Kate shivered. They had reached the front steps, a wide fan of marble that led up to two large doors. She glanced at Nick. "Don't be coy, okay?"

Nick's low laughter did nothing to alleviate Kate's goose bumps. "How many people live in this house?" she asked abruptly.

Nick shrugged. "It varies, I guess."

Kate followed him up. His evasive answer did nothing to dull the apprehension that was rising in her.

A burst of warm air interrupted her thoughts. The door had opened as if by magic, revealing a straight-backed gentleman in a dark suit. He had gray hair that was so perfectly coiffed Kate was sure each strand had been set individually in place.

"Hello, Carlton," Nick said.

"Back so soon, Mr. Bannister?" The man kept his eyes focused on Nick, carefully avoiding Kate's presence at his side.

"Had a bit of an accident." Nick glanced down at his sleeve and smiled. "But my friend Kate got the worst of it."

Carlton lifted thick, bushy silver brows and looked at Kate. Kate suppressed a grin. Carlton was trying hard to keep his face impassive and not register utter dismay at her appearance, but he was failing miserably.

"We had a little problem on a slick hill," Nick offered in explanation, leading the way to the staircase.

"I see." Carlton's brows lowered slightly. "Trouble on a slick hill," he repeated to himself as if forcing sense into the words.

"Miss Morelli needs to use one of the guest rooms to clean up a little."

"I see, sir." Carlton gave Kate a slight nod and began a slow, careful climb of the steps.

Kate began to follow him, then glanced back at Nick. He was standing at the bottom, his arm resting on the banister, a curious look of enjoyment lighting his eyes.

Kate shivered again. This was a very strange predicament to be in, she thought, but at the moment upstairs seemed far less dangerous than walking back down to Nick Bannister. Kate focused on Carlton's ramrod-straight back and continued her ascent.

Carlton led Kate into a suite of rooms that nearly equalled the size of her whole apartment. The bedroom was lovely, with soft cream carpeting and blue flowered wallpaper. The bed was wide and high, covered with an elegant blue-and-gold spread. Kate slipped out of her shoes. "This is lovely, Carlton, but all I really need is a bathroom and a few old rags so I can—"

But Carlton wasn't listening. He had moved into an adjacent room and before Kate could follow him, she heard the sound of a shower running.

He returned almost as quickly as he had disappeared, this time carrying an armload of soft towels. He carefully set them on a long bench at the foot of the bed, then lifted a white terry-cloth robe from behind the closet door.

"Thank you, Carlton," Kate tried again. "This is very hospitable of you, but I don't need a shower. I—"

"Miss?" Carlton's brows had lifted again and the message in that movement stilled her. She looked down at her suit. It was perfectly clear that in Carlton's eyes she most certainly *did* need a shower, and the sooner the better.

"While you are freshening up, we will attempt to clean off your clothing, miss."

Kate started to object. And then she realized it was futile. So she nodded, grabbed a towel and disappeared into the steamy depths of the bathroom.

Four

—

If only she could bottle and sell Carlton. It seemed to Kate he had thought of everything.

When she emerged from the shower, she found a pair of buttercup-yellow warm-ups lying across the bed and her muddied suit gone. She dried herself and dressed quickly. The sweats were comfortable and warm, obviously feminine. Whose? Kate shook her head and dismissed the niggling curiosity. Who cared whose? They were on her now. Nick Bannister's private life was certainly not her affair.

She looked around. In addition to the clothes, Carlton had set out a hairbrush and comb next to her purse and he had left a small pot of hot tea on a nearby table. It was a life one could get accustomed to without much effort at all.

She ran the comb through her still damp hair, then stepped out into the hallway and closed the bedroom door behind her. Guest room or not, she felt slightly uncomfortable lounging in one of Nick Bannister's boudoirs. She needed to be on her way.

There was a stillness in the hallway that astonished her at first. Kate's apartment building was never quiet, not early in the morning, not late at night. And when people weren't making the noise that seeped through the paper-thin walls, then the traffic on busy Wornall Road was. She stood still for a minute and listened to the silence before glancing down toward the end of the hall. And then she saw Carlton standing straight and alert beside a large urn near the top of the stairs.

"This way, miss," he said without turning his head. Kate hesitated for a fraction of a second. This way to where? It had been such a peculiar few hours that practically anything was possible. But she didn't need any more excitement. She was clean and dry; what she needed now were her clothes and a polite exit. Maybe Nick had already left for his social event and she could somehow retrieve her suit and slip out the door and back into her sane, ordinary life.

"Miss?" Carlton's brows were drawing together above his eyes. Kate imagined a fat, furry caterpillar nestling there. She blinked away the thought and walked toward him.

Carlton led her silently down the staircase and into the library. Her heart did an unexpected somersault. Nick was still very much present. He was sitting on a leather couch, a pipe in his hand. He had removed his jacket, but it didn't change his appearance much. He still looked elegant and untouchable. Soft lights fell across his still form, telling Kate that she had stayed in the shower far longer than she intended. Daylight had disappeared a while ago.

"It's late," she said, abruptly announcing her presence. "You have things to do and so do I. Thanks for everything. Are my clothes handy?"

Nick looked up at the staccato sound of her words. His smile came only after he had seen her and then he stood. "No need to rush off. Your clothes aren't quite ready."

"But your party—"

He shrugged.

Kate didn't know what her next move was, so she opted for idle talk. "What is it, anyway, this thing you were on your way to?"

"Cocktail buffet."

"It must be an elegant buffet." Again she took in the long length of him in the crisp white shirt broken only by the line of suspenders. "Well, I mean the tux and all—"

"The Bolshoi ballet is here tonight. It's a beautiful performance and dinner is part of the festivities. Since it was being held at a neighbor's, I decided to walk over."

"Oh, sure." Kate half smiled. And then she added, "I should have remembered, about the ballet, I mean. All our limos are busy tonight because of it."

"Good," Nick said. He didn't know what to say next, a most unusual situation for him when he was with a woman. He didn't want her to leave, and there was absolutely no reason for her to stay. "How about dinner?" he asked suddenly. "I owe you one."

"Owe me? That's silly. What makes you think that?"

"You fed me the other night."

"You don't owe me anything. That dinner was an attempt to talk to you about my business proposal, pure and simple. And it failed. Failed business attempts don't require reciprocation." She hadn't intended to bring up this bone of contention between them right now, not after his hospitality. But once again her mouth had opened and out had come the words, a condition that often plagued Kate.

Nick frowned. "What do you mean?"

"St. Anthony's Hospital, the board, my limo-service proposal. You know." Why did she always say everything that came into her head? This was not the right time to discuss this, not when he was being such a good host. She bit down hard on her bottom lip and fought to control herself. But the anger connected with his rejection of her proposal was still there, percolating just beneath the surface. As she stood thinking about it, it slowly flowed back, prickling the back of her neck. And she was suddenly too tired to deal with any of it. She simply wanted to go home. She fought against the feelings and concentrated on the manners her mother had painstakingly tried to instill in her.

"Look," she said, "I appreciate your kindness, the shower and all. And I don't want to get into a business discussion with you. I just want to go home."

"At least sit long enough to tell me what you're talking about."

Kate's anger was now mixed with confusion. And then it registered. Nick Bannister was such a big-shot businessman that the deal with St. Anthony's was small potatoes, so small, in fact, that he didn't even remember squelching a deal that would have granted her company a taste of financial security.

Kate lowered herself into an overstuffed chair near the fireplace. She stared into the flames for a minute, then looked back at Nick. "I own a small com pany—" she began with exaggerated calm.

"Of course you do. I know that. The Morelli Limo Company. Great cars, by the way."

"Thank you." He was a puzzlement, she thought, looking into his clear blue eyes to see if he was putting her on. It didn't seem so. "Well, if you remember the company, perhaps you can dredge up the memory of vetoing my plan for St. Anthony's Hospital. I believe the meeting was held yesterday?"

Nick looked at Kate intently. It was a look that pushed away the anger in her. She could almost see his mind working, piecing together the parts of what she was saying. Just from watching his face, she was able to understand part of his success.

And then his expression changed. The parts were in place and a look of understanding softened the harder lines. "Of course, the board meeting. You'll have to excuse my forgetfulness. It's been a hectic couple of days. Lots going on at work, these incessant board meetings, social things... For a minute I didn't connect." He laughed.

It was a mellow kind of laughter that didn't fit the Nick Bannister who was sitting in front of her, resplendent in his custom-made tuxedo, nor the Nick who appeared in the society pages with his gorgeous companions. Her cousin Maria had once told her of seeing a picture of Nick at a glamorous party in Antibes or somewhere just as exotic. He was an international playboy, Maria had added, sighing.

"I guess maybe I work *too* hard at leaving business behind," Nick was saying. "But anyway, now I remember."

Kate waited for the cool, businesslike explanation.

"About that meeting," he said. "I'm really ashamed to say I don't know the outcome of it—"

"What do you mean?"

"I couldn't attend, so I called Sister Maria, told her you and I had talked and that I was convinced you could do the job. She agreed and said she hoped she could convince Cyrus Hodges. He doesn't much like fancy amenities, and the whole limo idea was a little too luxurious for his taste." Nick shook his head. "I don't think he likes kids much, either. Maybe not even pregnant women."

"Hodges . . ." Kate's single word hung in the air.

"Well, he's from the old school, Kate. Lived through the Depression and still thinks that way. Unnecessary expenses bother him, and I guess he viewed the limo service in that light. His mother probably had her kids in the back bedroom of their house and went to work in the family store the next day."

A rush of unexpected pleasure coursed through Kate. She felt it in her limbs, across her shoulders, followed by the inevitable color rising and spreading across her cheeks. "So you didn't blackball me, after all?"

"Blackball you?" Nick leaned forward, his elbows resting on his knees and his intense blue eyes focusing on her face. "Listen, Kate, anyone who can serve a meal like that in the back of a limo can run a company. I take my meals very seriously."

Kate felt giddy.

"I can see from the look on your face that Sister Maria must have been successful in convincing Hodges. Great. I'm glad you got the business."

"No, no actually we didn't get it. I guess Cyrus held his ground."

"But—"

Kate waved her hands in the air. "But it doesn't matter. We sold the idea to another hospital—St. Joseph's."

"Well good. Good for you, I mean, bad for St. Anthony's. So we have something to celebrate. That's great." He called out for Carlton, and Kate was amazed at how fast the older man appeared.

"Carlton, Miss Morelli is staying for dinner. And we'll need to be chilling some champagne, as well."

"Dinner, sir?" Carlton's long face was fighting to hide surprise.

"Yes. And you'll have to call the Sutherlands and express my sincere regrets for missing their party."

"As you wish, sir. And dinner, sir?"

"Tell Shelly to make anything that's easy. I'm sure she has something that she can dish up without much trouble."

"Yes, sir."

Kate listened with half an ear. She was still trying to make sense out of what she was doing. It had occurred to her somewhere in the middle of Nick and Carlton's conversation that she was still pleasantly full from the bratwurst. That what she really needed was sleep—she was exhausted. And that Nick had previous plans. But none of these facts moved her to action. Instead she sat in the soft, comfortable chair and watched Nick and his butler planning something—for her! Definitely crazy. What was it Harry always said? *Carpe diem?* Or some such thing. Okay, she'd do it. She'd seize the day. And then she'd tuck it away and pull it out when she wanted to relive the fantasy—of Kate Morelli being served dinner by a butler named Carlton in Mr. Nicholas Bannister's fine mansion. The thought brought a smile to her lips that was so broad both Nick and Carlton turned to look at her. Nick returned the smile, then turned back to Carlton.

"Just one more thing, Carlton," he said. "No need to rush dinner. We're not going any place."

"But—" Kate started to remind him of the ballet, but bit back the rest of the sentence. Nicholas Bannister didn't need her to remind him of his engagements. He had a very efficient secretary to do that.

"Ballet isn't one of my favorite art forms," he said, reading her face. "And I won't be missed."

Kate doubted that, then wondered if it meant he didn't have a date. He usually did, at least according to cousin Maria. Nick Bannister had more women at his beck and call than Grandma Morelli had cats, Maria had said. He was noticeably present at every society event, she said, the most eligible bachelor in Kansas City. She had said it all with such awe that Kate had half expected her cousin to suggest she frame the contract she had with Worldwide Systems. Kate wondered with some pleasure what Maria would say when she heard about tonight.

When Kate tuned back in to the present, Carlton had disappeared and she could hear his footsteps fading away as they clicked rhythmically on the marble hallway floor. She and Nick were alone, and he was sitting back in his chair, his long legs stretched out in front of him. He looked relaxed, handsome and far sexier than she would have liked.

"So," Nick said, placing his hands behind his head, "here we are."

Kate sighed.

"Hungry?" Nick asked, misreading the sound.

Kate shook her head. "I ate not long ago. I should have told you before."

"No problem. You can drink champagne while I eat. I'm starved."

"You should have gone on to the dinner. You could have, you know."

"Oh, I know."

A slight smile accompanied his response and Kate shivered. Of course he knew. Nick Bannister did as he pleased. Kate sighed again.

"What's the matter?"

"Nothing, that's what's the matter. I have nothing to say to you. I don't know why I'm here. I *shouldn't* be, you know. And I don't know why *you're* here, instead of where you should be."

"Hey, Kate, there're too many shoulds in your conversation. Should's put a horrible strain on life."

"They also give it some definition, some purpose."

Nick shrugged. "That depends on your philosophy, I guess. But if you insist on reasons for all this, I can give you some easy ones." He smiled lazily. "You're here because you needed to clean up, and I'm here because I happened to be in the park and wanted to help. And we're both here because I don't like ballet and you're one of the loveliest excuses to tumble down the hill in front of me in quite some time. It's fate, Kate, pure and simple. So why not relax a little and enjoy it?"

"I am relaxed," Kate said quickly.

"Okay, good. Would you like a drink?"

Kate looked around the room, then focused back on Nick. "Actually, what I'd really like is a tour of this house. It's the biggest home I've ever seen." And moving around looking at grand things was a far easier task than sitting in the quiet room with Nick Bannister.

"Yeah, it is a big place," Nick said. "Sure, I'd be glad to show you around." He stood and nodded toward the door. "Shall we?"

Kate was in awe as they passed through a dining room that could easily seat twenty-five, an enormous living room that was so elegant and proper Kate suspected it was never used, a den, an office, a sunroom and a greenhouse, a playroom and so many bedrooms she began to lose count.

"How many people live here?" she finally asked again as they descended from a third-floor ballroom.

"Just me."

Kate stopped dead in her tracks on the thickly carpeted step. She wanted to laugh. She didn't know who else she thought lived there, but certainly there had to be a whole bevy of relatives or friends stashed away somewhere. No one would live alone in a house the size of a small hotel. "That's the most ridiculous thing I ever heard," she said, more to herself than to Nick.

"What?"

Kate resumed walking. "I was just wondering why a bachelor would live in a house like this. It doesn't make sense to me."

Nick shrugged. "Because it was here. And it was easier than selling it and finding somewhere else to live. I was raised in this house and my parents, sister...and others...have long since moved away."

"But it's so huge."

"I never thought much about it, I guess. I'm not here all the time. I've got other places I can go to if I want something cozier."

"Other places?"

"Apartments. Condos, that kind of thing. Most are owned by the company."

"Where? I mean the condos, where are they?" She knew Maria would ask.

"They're in Aspen, Key Largo, New York, places like that."

"I see." But she didn't really see. She knew there were people who lived that way. She didn't wear blinders. And a lot of them were customers of hers. It was just that no one she *knew* lived this way, so what was she doing here, anyway? She followed Nick down another flight of stairs. "Well," she said, trying not to be judgmental, "I guess it's a case of each to his own. I couldn't live in a house big enough to host a convention, but you can. So that's fine." She smiled brightly with a show of indulgence.

Nick laughed. "You're something else, Kate Morelli. Most women are *impressed* with this place, believe it or not."

"Well, Nick," she said seriously, "most women probably *came* here to be impressed, not to wash mud off their noses. Now, how are you at pool?"

They were standing at the door of the most elaborate recreation room Kate had ever seen. A pool table, its sides polished to such a gleam that they reflected her face, held center stage.

"You play pool?" Nick asked, one brow lifted dubiously.

"Ask me that after a game or two." Carefully she lifted a cue stick from the wooden holder on the mahogany-paneled walls and squinted slightly as she measured its weight.

Just then Carlton appeared out of nowhere with a bottle of champagne chilling in a silver bucket, and he proceeded to uncork it without uttering a word.

"Now how did he know to do that?" Kate asked in wonderment after the butler left.

"Training," Nick said, chalking the end of his cue stick.

"And practice, I suppose," Kate added, not bothering to hide the insinuation behind her words.

"I suppose," Nick said with a laugh. He poured two glasses and handed her one. "To the game of pool—and to beautiful, unexpected guests," he said, clinking her glass.

Kate felt the rosy glow spread across her cheeks and hid it behind the champagne. She took a long, cooling drink and savored the tingling liquid as it created a lovely warm pathway down her throat. She held the glass out in front of her and looked at the bubbles rising to the top. "I don't drink much, you know. Almost never, really. But this tastes very good tonight," she admitted sincerely.

"I'm glad you like it," he said after a moment's silence, as if he had been pondering her words.

Kate put down her glass and circled the table, then bent gracefully over the flat field of green felt. She placed her stick against the cue ball and expertly sent it rolling across the table.

While Nick watched in amazement, the collection of balls scattered, four of them sailing neatly into pockets. "There," was all Kate said, her pleasure obvious in the blush that tinged her cheeks.

"Touché," Nick said, and took his turn.

When it was Kate's turn again, Nick leaned against the oak bar, sipped his champagne and let the sight of this pool-playing wisp of a woman tease his senses. She was certainly an enigma, and he found that watching her brought him an intense pleasure. Her hair was still damp from the shower and it curled around her face. She wore no makeup, but her face was glowing. She was totally oblivious of her natural beauty, a fact Nick found both surprising and exciting. He didn't know any women like that.

When the game ended in Kate's favor, the usually competitive Nick felt a sweet rush at the obvious joy her victory brought her. "You're terrific, Kate! Where did you learn to play like that?" He handed her a fresh glass of champagne.

Kate was flushed, and her heart was beating faster than usual. She took a quick sip of the wine. "My father taught me when I was a kid. And Harry and I have a never-ending tournament so I stay in shape."

"What else do you play?"

The innocent question took on an unexpected tone, and Kate felt the same unease that had nearly suffocated her that night in the limo when she had valiantly denied the desire stirred by Nick's presence. She took another sip of the champagne and tried to corral her feelings.

Nick felt the air charged by his words. And just as quickly, he felt her guard go up and he regretted speaking at all. Kate's wonderful spontaneity had filled the room with warmth and life, and he didn't want to restrain it by making her uncomfortable. "I didn't mean anything by that, Kate. Honest. Come on, let's eat." He took her elbow and led her out of the pool room.

They walked quietly, quickly, up the wide stairs and through the front hall. Kate didn't say a word. There was no way on God's green earth she would let herself give in to her feelings for Nick. No, not Kate Morelli. Sure, Nick was handsome and sexy as all get-out. But her body was playing tricks on her, that was all. And she could handle her body's tricks. Concentration, that was all it would take.

Kate and Nick went back to the library where new logs had been added to the fire to ward off the fall chill. It was dark beyond the windows now, but the room was warm and cheery and the air was filled with the tantalizing aroma of basil and garlic. Kate followed the aroma and looked over to the far side of the room where Carlton stood next to a glass-topped cart. He was mixing fettuccine in a huge bowl. A fresh bottle of wine stood open on the massive oak coffee table and two glasses reflected the firelight. Kate headed for the fire and Nick poured two glasses. He held one out to Kate.

"Here's to you, Kate. And to the success of your business."

Kate realized that was a bit of niceness in him, too. Here he was, neutralizing things, helping her past that embarrassing moment down in the pool room. She didn't know what had gotten into her, but in that instant she had wanted to touch Nick Bannister, to feel the smooth silk of his tuxedo, to measure the wide, flat span of his chest with her fingers. It was crazy, uncharacteristic. Kate Morelli was many things, but seductress was not in her repertoire. And never would be, thanks to the lessons taught so effectively by one Gregory Hutton.

With that resolution in place, Kate took a long swallow of wine while Nick watched her in surprise.

"Kate, ah, are you sure you don't want anything to eat?"

"Absolutely." She smiled and curled up on the sofa. "But you sit right down here and eat and don't worry about me." She patted the cushion next to her.

As soon as Nick was seated, Carlton placed a gold-rimmed plate, heaped with fettuccine in a rich aromatic sauce, on the coffee table in front of him. Nick pulled his bow tie off and tossed it onto the end of the couch, then undid the top buttons of his starched white shirt and eyed the food. He sighed contentedly. "Carlton, this is great."

"Here's to Carlton," Kate said, holding her glass up to the butler.

"Ma'am," Carlton said with a slight nod of his head and then disappeared.

"He's a veritable Houdini, the way he disappears," Kate commented. She giggled, imagining Carlton on a stage, performing magic tricks.

Nick felt her giggle deep down inside him. It was a musical sound, a medley of silver bells, and the echo stayed with him even after her laughter had stopped. He shook his head and concentrated on the fettuccine.

"So tell me about yourself, Nicholas Bannister," Kate said. She was snuggled into the corner of the couch, her feet tucked beneath her, her body nicely warmed by the wine and the fire. She no longer felt frightened or uncomfortable with this man. She knew now she could handle anything.

Nick looked at her, noting how soft and vulnerable she appeared. There was none of the bravado he had seen in her at other times. "There's not much to tell.

Besides, I think I pale next to you in the interest department."

Kate ignored his evasive tactic. "Why aren't you married, Nick? And kids, my lord, you could have seventeen in this house and still have room for more. They could roller-skate in the front hall!"

"Seventeen kids?"

"Well, maybe just seven or so. Too many and you wouldn't have time to be a good father to each and run your business. Personally I'm going to have five, unless of course the limo company makes me extremely wealthy and I could afford to raise more."

"Will there be a husband?"

Kate held out her glass for a refill. "A husband? Oh, for the kids." She laughed. "Of course there will be a husband. A gentle, warm, intelligent man who will share the duties of parenthood right down the middle. Fifty-fifty. That's how my pop did it. Of course there was only me, so the duties weren't stupendous or anything."

"I see." Nick nodded in answer to the intense look she was giving him that seemed to expect an answer. He suspected raising Kate Morelli had been a formidable task and a respect for her father began to grow in him. "Tell me about your father, Kate."

"Pop?" She smiled and her face grew soft. "My mother and pop were wonderful."

Nick wondered about how her parents died but before he could ask, Kate went on.

"We had the best times, the best family. My parents would have liked a whole houseful of kids, but they made the best of it, of just having me. We had aunts and uncles and cousins all over the place, though, so I never really considered myself an only child. Not until—''

She paused for such a long time that Nick thought she had lost her train of thought, forgotten what she was talking about. She sat there drinking her champagne and thinking. Just as Nick was about to speak she began again and there was tremendous sorrow in her voice. "I never felt like an only child until they died. Then, even with all the aunts and uncles and cousins, I felt so much aloneness I thought I would die, too." She looked at Nick and her eyes were so large he thought he would drown in them. "They were at my aunt and uncle's that night, at a surprise birthday party for Uncle Morrie—he had one every year, as regular as clockwork. And then Mom and Pop went home and that was when he hit them. And he—or she—never stayed around, just left them there in the crumpled car."

Nick had never seen such sadness. Without thought, he reached out and touched her shoulder.

Kate sighed deeply, her eyes on the fire. When she looked back at Nick the sadness was softer, more manageable.

"How long ago?" he asked.

"A couple of years. Yesterday. It's hard to put it into time, you know?"

Nick smiled and rubbed her shoulder absently. He didn't know, not really. Because Nick had never loved that way, enough for it to make a difference in his life. He couldn't really imagine loving anyone that much. For a second he shifted uncomfortably, realizing that when his own father had died what he had felt was not sadness but relief.

Kate took a sip of her wine. "I don't know why I'm doing this, Nick. I don't usually talk so much about things that are so . . . so personal. Maybe it's because I don't really know you. I think sometimes it's easier to talk to strangers."

"I'm not a stranger, Kate."

Kate smiled. "No, I guess not. Not anymore. Our lives seem to be overlapping, don't they."

Nick liked the thought of that—of overlapping his life on Kate's for a brief time. That wasn't his way normally, to let his life be touched in that way, but the concept, coming from Kate's mouth, was appealing.

Kate lifted her glass. "Here's to overlapping lives."

"To overlapping lives," Nick murmured, filling his glasses again.

"So now, Nick Bannister," Kate said, settling back against the cushions, "you have sideswiped—" She giggled and covered her mouth with her hand, then continued, "no, *sidestepped* me again. I still know nothing about this house, about you, about—" she shrugged and gave him a small smile "—about what it is about you that makes me glad to see you again." Kate knew as she said the words she'd not only regret them later, but would never have said them if the wine had not given her courage. "So," she added quickly, "why aren't you married?"

"Now I like that. No beating around the bush. Straightforward questions."

His voice was serious, but Kate could see the smile in his dark blue eyes. She leaned her head against the pillows, her eyes staying on his face. "Some would call it impertinent."

"And if I might take a wild guess, you've been called that once or twice?"

"Oh, and much worse." Kate grinned. The thing that astounded her the most was that she was having fun. Having fun with Nick Bannister was something she'd never have imagined just a few days before, but here she was, curled up contentedly right next to him, feeling as if they were old school friends.

"Whatever you call it, a straightforward question deserves a like answer. I'm not married because I have a genetic deficiency that makes marriage impossible."

Kate's face screwed up comically as she tried in earnest to make sense out of his words.

"It's not worth that much thought," he said, "All I meant is that I was married once, and before the divorce was ever final, I faced up to the fact that I'm not the marrying kind. No one in my family is. My parents were divorced when I was young, my sister has been married and divorced three times and she's only the ripe old age of twenty-nine. The first time was when she was sixteen and she ran off with our house painter because she was mad as hell at my father about something or another. Anyway, I could go on and on with aunts and uncles and cousins. The Bannister family is not at all like the Morellis, Kate. Marriage to us is an occasion for lots of parties, then shortly after, a quick trip to Mexico for the divorce, and therapy bills." He watched her take another sip of her wine as she thought about what he was saying.

"I see." Kate's mind lingered on how he'd been married before. She probably should have known that, since it more than likely had dominated the gossip mills for some time. But then, she hadn't really paid much attention to things like that. "Who was she?" she asked out loud, and then realized the rudeness of her question. "Hey, I'm sorry I asked that. It's none of my business, and she certainly isn't anyone I'd know anyway. Here's to not asking impertinent questions." She held up her glass and touched the rim of Nick's, then took a drink.

"It wasn't rude, Kate. But it doesn't matter who she was, because it was a stab at something that should never have been. I think both Elizabeth—that was her name—and I knew that. But she had things she wanted from it, and I thought foolishly that if I married 'right,' maybe I could dispel the family curse." He shrugged. "I was wrong for a change."

"And eating humble pie is not your forte I can tell."

"Nope, it's not." Nick took a long sip of wine and played with the fact that Kate Morelli was the first person to whom he had mentioned Elizabeth's name after she had left. The whole experience had been so distressing he had buried it deep inside him and refused to let it surface. Until tonight.

"Did she live here in this house?"

"Yes. She liked the house, and that was about it. She didn't like me, and she hated Kansas City. It was a great relief to her when she went back to Boston."

Kate was having trouble thinking of Nick living here with a wife. The image kept fading, shifting out of focus as if it didn't belong. Trying to concentrate on the conversation, she shifted and her knee lightly touched Nick's thigh. She smiled at him. "You'll find another wife, Nick. Don't you worry."

"I'm not," he replied, wondering at the small fire her touch had lit in him. "And I won't. Find another wife I mean."

Kate continued to sip her champagne. Finally she said, "You have a nice voice, Nick."

"Well thank you, m'lady. And you are a nice dinner companion." Hell, what was going on here? The woman must be part witch. Strong, heated sensations stroked his limbs.

"Shh." Kate pressed two fingers against his lips. "Listen. Do you hear it?"

The sound reaching his ears the loudest was his heartbeat, pounding noisily in his chest.

"It's the sound of night," she said softly. "The deepest sound of all." Her head was now inches away, her hand had slipped down and was resting lightly on his chest, one finger looped beneath the black band of his suspenders.

"Hey, Kate..." There was a gruffness in his voice that belied the feelings clouding his reason. "If you don't watch out—"

Kate tilted her head so her lips were only a hair's breadth from his. "If I don't watch out, what?"

"Then I'm going to have to kiss you."

"Now?" She moved closer to him until their thighs touched. Her lips were slightly opened and her eyes watched him.

Nick didn't answer. It would have been useless. He closed the small amount of remaining space between them and met her lips with great hunger. When his tongue slipped inside her mouth, her response was immediate. Her breasts now pressed into his chest, and he felt how soft and warm and wonderful she was. An enormous wave of desire flooded him.

Kate stirred.

Nick pulled back and searched her face. It was beautiful, full of longing and the same yearning that filled him. Nick sucked in a lungful of breath and steadied himself. He wanted her. God, how he wanted her. But he had to force himself to think.

Kate was obviously slightly looped, the result of too many glasses of champagne that he had readily poured for her. He knew that was why she was acting this way with him. And in spite of what the gossip mongers said, Nick Bannister did not take advantage of women.

"What...?" Kate's eyes opened. Cool air moved across her face.

Nick smiled halfheartedly.

"I liked that, Nick."

"That goes without saying."

Kate tried to focus on what was happening. She was trying to seduce Nick Bannister, that was what was happening. "Oh, Nick," she whispered.

"What?"

Kate fought for clarity, but everything seemed fuzzy. Water. She needed cold water on her face. That would wake her, bring order to all this. "The ladies' room?" she asked.

"Oh, sure." Nick was up in a second and helped her stand. He pointed her toward a door just outside the library.

"Back in a jiffy," Kate said and then disappeared as quickly as her shaking legs could carry her.

Nick poured himself a glass of brandy and slumped back down onto the sofa. He took a long drink, then rested his head on the cushions. What had he almost done? Another minute of Kate Morelli and he would have had her up in his bedroom. She had cast a spell on him, and although Nick had often escorted women to his bed, reason seemed to have nothing to do with this. He had almost lost control. He squeezed his eyes shut, then forced himself to relax. The fire in his loins was dying now. Kate Morelli, the most unlikely of conquests. Even the word didn't fit her. In her normal state, Nick felt sure Kate would be nobody's conquest. She was definitely her own woman.

The brandy curled down inside of him and his body began to relax. Slow, lovely thoughts of Kate wandered across his mind. She had felt good in his arms, utterly desirable. Nick sighed and let the thoughts take over him completely.

It was a half hour later when Kate felt ready to emerge from the elegant rest room off the entry foyer.

Water hadn't helped much, so Kate had opened the small window to let the night air clear her senses. It hadn't helped much, either, so she had sat on the small, cushioned chaise until she felt somewhat better. She'd go back to the den now and suggest to Nick that he take her home. She looked into the mirror and practiced, opening her eyes wide and speaking very carefully. "Thank you for a lovely time..." Surely she could handle that. She opened the door and walked carefully across the hall. She could see the fireplace and the couch...and Nick's head resting on the pillows. She took a deep breath and began, "I thank you for the wonderful time..."

A large figure stood a few feet away in the shadows and turned toward Kate at the sound of her voice.

Kate looked at Carlton and grinned. "Hi, there," she said.

"Good evening, madame. I believe that Mr. Bannister has fallen asleep."

"Asleep," Kate repeated.

"Do you wish to be driven home?"

Kate nodded. "And let's let the master sleep."

"Certainly, madame."

In moments Kate was seated in the back of a town car with Carlton's gray head directly in front of her. Patiently he helped Kate remember her address, then urged her to sit back and relax. He assured her she would soon be home.

"It was lovely, Carlton," she said closing her eyes.

"Yes, miss."

"Mr. Bannister is a wonderful man." An image of Nick in his black suspenders with crisp white shirt. And then she thought of Nick in black suspenders with nothing underneath. "He is a perfect gentleman," she said with sincerity. "He's a gentleman, Carlton, and you're a gentleman."

"Yes, miss," said Carlton.

"And it was right to leave, because otherwise... you understand, don't you Carlton?"

"Yes, miss."

"I'm not that way, Carlton," Kate went on. "No, I'm not. But Mr. Bannister is so handsome and sexy." She thought of his broad chest, and felt a surge of pleasure warm her. "I wanted to keep kissing him." She allowed a small laugh to float around the car. "Heck, Carlton, I wanted a lot more than that!"

Carlton coughed.

"But it wouldn't have been right, Carlton. No, not that way."

Carlton drove on in silence. A short while later, he pulled up in front of her four-storey apartment house. "Ma'am?"

Kate was silent.

"Miss Morelli, we're home. I shall escort you in-side."

She saw Carlton slowly turn around and look at her just before she fell asleep.

Five

___

Two weeks wasn't usually a long time in Kate's busy life. Her days were always crammed full of things to do. She was always, as Harry often told her, a day late and a dollar short.

But the two weeks following the evening she spent at Nick Bannister's house stretched like the Great Wall of China across the tender surface of her heart.

She missed Nick terribly. When he called, she avoided speaking to him, of course. Why put herself into the frying pan when there was absolutely only one possible result? No, Kate Morelli might be emotional and romantic and impressionable at times, but she definitely wasn't foolish. There had already been some damage done emotionally. The Morelli Limo Company was having to share her concentration with another entity. That wasn't fair, but Kate couldn't do anything about it. Nick was there in her thoughts, wedged tightly between her plans for St. Joseph's Hospital maternity service and the American Royal Botar Ball, which would be a boon for business.

"Hey," Harry said, "why don't you just talk to the guy?"

"At least you've given up on making me feel we were biting the hand that feeds us."

"That, too," Harry said wisely.

"Harry, he's out of this world, and I mean that literally. He's out of my world socially, economically, historically, probably politically!"

Harry shrugged. "Little things."

"No, Harry dear. Big things. Huge things. I want someone constant, not handsome and rich."

"The three are incompatible?"

"In this case, yes. Nick Bannister is a nice person—sometimes. At least he can be nice for three hours. That might be his limit, I don't know. But he has no real interest in me, Harry. He's used to big-time women who give black-tie buffets. No, I know enough about that world. It's not for me."

Kate had learned too much about that other world, and though she often made mistakes, she tried not to make the same one twice. She shivered as she thought back to the summer she met Gregory Hutton.

Nick didn't look like Gregory, nor did the two act alike. But appearances weren't what made her heart ache. She had met Gregory in England at Paddington Station; she was lost and he was her knight in shining armor, certainly the stuff romances were made of. And he had escorted her around London, squiring her to theaters and restaurants and country homes until her head was spinning and her heart was swollen with the excess of it all. He was fun and dashing and even had titles in his family tree, and when he told Kate he loved her, her twenty-four-year-old heart sang and allowed him to take her off to his four-hundred-year-old bed, upon which barons and dukes and princesses had also slept.

The end of their romance was predictable in hindsight, but Kate hadn't seen it coming at all. Gregory had been her first great love. And when the dizziness she had been feeling turned into a pregnancy, she was frightened but not terrified. They loved each other, after all. It would be all right. But the day after she told him, she found the engraved envelope on her pillow. She had numbly fingered the crisp bank notes that accompanied Gregory's farewell message, and her heart had crumbled into a million pieces.

Weeks later she couldn't be sure what had caused the painful miscarriage—her emotional devastation or simply fate—but when she returned home to Kansas City after it was all over, she knew she was not the same woman who previously had plunged so wholeheartedly and foolishly into life. In spite of the huge sorrow she felt, Kate had been able to see through it to learn something. Kate had learned extreme caution. Men of Gregory Hutton's ilk—handsome playboys with money and possessions that were boundless—did not make good husbands and fathers.

And that was really what she, Kate Morelli, wanted. Once her business was thriving to the point that she could hear Frank Morelli whispering in her ear, "A stupendous job, my bambina. You did me proud," then she could concentrate on just that, on finding a good, dependable husband and having children who would also have made their grandpop proud.

"So, Morelli, what'll it be?"

"Huh?" Kate jerked her head up.

"Huh? Huh? Do I look like a *huh*?" Harry leaned over and planted a big kiss on her forehead. "Fresh air, babe. That's what you need. And I need to pick up the major for a big shindig. So, I'm off."

Kate, still daydreaming, only half heard Harry, and then he was gone and the barrage of paperwork and ringing telephone jerked her back into the harsh reality of the day.

By five she was exhausted but contented with the thought that she had pushed Nick Bannister out of her mind for nearly three hours. She'd go home and shower off the tiredness and settle down to read a mystery.

The phone rang as she pushed out the chair.

For a minute she thought about letting the answering machine get it. But the ringing got to her and she picked it up to hear a frantic female voice begging for a ride.

"Ma'am," Kate said calmly, "I think you have the wrong number."

The caller insisted she had the right number; Morelli Limo Company was what she wanted. "There's a woman here in my store about to give birth. I can't leave the store, there's not a cab in sight and a man said to call you, that you do business with St. Joseph's Hospital. That's where she says she wants to go, but you'd better come quick or the hospital isn't going to get *this* business." The woman rattled off the address of a small shop on the Plaza just a few blocks away, and hung up.

Kate stared at the phone, a part of her wondering if someone was pulling her leg. She picked up the keys to the Grand Knight, the only car left in the shop. She was leaving anyway. She might as well drive by. What if it were a board member or a spouse of one and she failed to help out? And even if it weren't, Kate couldn't leave this poor woman in the lurch like that. She rushed out the door and sped to the shop.

There wasn't a parking place in front, so Kate double-parked and laid on the horn. A flurry of activity greeted the sound. In seconds the back car door had opened and closed, and Nick Bannister's head looked through the partially open partition. "Hi."

"You conniving, dishonest—" Kate clenched her teeth together."

"Desperate, needy—"

"This is ridiculous!"

"Agreed. To the airport, please. The Municipal, downtown."

Kate was fuming. The man was certifiably crazy. She ought to be taking him over to Western Missouri Mental Health Clinic! A horn blared behind her.

"You're causing a traffic jam."

"I'd like to jam you. Why didn't you just call a cab if you have a plane to catch? And what did you do, hire an actress to put on that little act over the phone?"

"If I had called myself you wouldn't have come. And no one was hired. It was a friend who called, at her suggestion. I didn't know she'd ham it up like that. Seems she has fantasies about being on stage."

"Ha. Well she better forget about it. It was low-budget horror-film acting at best."

"You came, didn't you?"

"Soft heart and superstition, that's what got me here."

"Why the hell won't you talk to me on the phone? I'm sorry I fell asleep on you, Kate, but I don't think it merits this kind of Alaskan freeze, do you? Couldn't you be overreacting just a bit?"

Kate pulled carefully into the line of traffic and headed downtown. She bit down hard on her bottom lip. She had been silly about not taking his calls. A phone conversation certainly didn't mean anything. It was just that her heart was acting so crazy. She reacted when she saw Nick, and it bothered her.

Nick went on. "I do apologize for the snooze, Kate. I guess it was the fire and the wine—and the fact that you seemed to be settling down for the night in the damn bathroom."

"Yeah, well, I'm sorry, too. I've been busy lately and just didn't get around to calling you back. What was it you wanted, anyway?"

"I wanted to see you again."

"Why?"

"Damned if I know! You're the most exasperating female I've ever met. But I did want to see you again. I do. Hey, watch out!"

Kate swerved to miss an orange cone that stood in the street beside a pothole. Nick slid against the door.

"Be careful."

"I told you you should have called a cab."

Nick ignored her comment. "When you cross the bridge, take the first turn into the airport."

"Yes, sir."

"I still owe you a dinner, you know."

"I drank enough champagne to equal quite a few dinners."

Nick chuckled. "Yeah, you did that."

Kate threw him a nasty look.

"Sorry. That was my fault. But you seemed to be enjoying yourself."

"Maybe that was the problem," Kate mumbled. She pulled the car into the airport entrance. "Where to?"

"Over there."

Following his directions, Kate pulled the limo around the hangar and stopped. "Okay, end of the line."

"Maybe it's just the beginning."

Kate looked back at Nick. He was smiling cryptically. "Come on, help me with this, will you?"

Kate glanced at the two packages he had brought with him. Reason said he could carry them himself. Professionalism said he was a customer and paying for her services. She got out of the car and stood there while Nick emerged from the back. He handed her one package, then took her elbow and guided her across the runway. "Everything ready, Pete?" he addressed a young-looking blond man who stood next to a small, sleek, private plane.

"All checked out and ready to go, Mr. B. Evening, miss." He bowed his head slightly.

"Hi," Kate said, mystified. They were acting funny, as if they knew something she didn't. Maybe it was the way Pete smiled. Her cousin Rudy used to do that after he had filled his sister's bedroom with mice.

"Kate, I have a confession to make."

Kate looked up at Nick. "Would you like me to drive you to church?"

"You're going with me. I'm finally taking you to dinner."

"And you're crazy." Kate turned and began to walk back to her car.

"It's all taken care of Kate. Harry said you were free tonight, and—"

Kate stopped and spun around. "Harry said? My Harry was in on this?"

"There's nothing to be in on. He just told me you didn't have plans. It's a simple dinner invitation. I'm not asking you to marry me."

"Thank heavens for small favors!" She paused and looked at the plane. "Dinner in a plane?"

"The plane will take us there." Nick had walked up close to her. "I'll have you back late tonight. We'll just have dinner, no strings attached. Honest."

Kate looked up into his striking blue eyes. And that, she knew immediately, was her undoing. "Now?" she said weakly.

"If we want to get there in time for our reservations."

"Oh," she said, as if it all made sense. When the blond pilot took the package from her hands and Nick took her arm, she simply went along, all the way up the stairs and into the small, posh airplane.

In one of the packages were fresh flowers for the low teak table, and the other contained hunks of imported cheese and several boxes of crackers. After Pete had taxied down the runway and the plane was airborne, a pleasant steward appeared from the shadows of a galley with a tray of the cheese and crackers and chilled glasses of wine. By the time they crossed over the Grand Canyon, Kate was chatting with Nick as if she flew across the country for dinner every night. And by the time they landed safely in San Francisco hours later, she was fully and completely settled into the fairy tale. For that was what it was—a fairy tale, pure and simple, and one couldn't begrudge a fairy tale, especially one that could be the topic of conversation during a dozen Sunday brunches with her family.

Nick stayed true to his word and remained the perfect gentleman. She was sure it wasn't the way he usually acted with women. And as they drove from the airport to a small, perfect restaurant above the wharf, Kate wondered briefly why he wasn't bored with her. Later when they watched the lights of the city dotting the black sky and the world seemed to be on a string that was tied to the end of her finger, Kate asked him.

"Why am I not bored with you?" Nick repeated. Then he sat back in the apricot-colored chair. "Kate, I could be a lot of things with you, but bored isn't one of them. There simply isn't a boring breath in your body."

"I like spinach and pot roast. I love old movies. I like to walk my dog. I don't mind sitting home on Saturday night and watching TV. I don't even mind sitting home alone. I'm boring, Nick."

"Okay, Kate, whatever you say," he said, and his eyes sparkled with disbelieving pleasure.

The flight back to Kansas City was as smooth as riding on a silken cloud and for the final hour, Kate rested her head on Nick's shoulder, closed her eyes and let the peace of the universe seep into her. She didn't really sleep; she replayed the evening and finally understood how Cinderella must have felt.

"You know," she said dreamily, "Cinderella may have had something there."

"Cinderella?"

Kate nodded. "I never liked that fairy tale much. I always thought Cinderella was selling out, that she should have found happiness or joy wherever she was, whatever walk of life. You shouldn't need wands or fairy godmothers and chariots for that. You know?''

"Mmm,'' Nick said, breathing in the wonderful scent of her hair.

"But tonight...well, now maybe I can see her point.'' She slipped back into her private thoughts. Sure, this changed things, this deep, velvety night that they were flying through, Nick at her side... Maybe she was too judgmental. And as Nick dropped tiny kisses across the top of her head, she decided definitely that she could excuse the blond cinder maid's folly. Being a princess for a while wasn't half bad.

Nick looked down at Kate, saw the smile on her face, and knew she wasn't asleep. But she was happy, that was clear, and had enjoyed the evening as much as he had. This was new, uncharted territory for Nick Bannister. He wasn't accustomed to feelings that expanded so greatly, that encompassed so much. They were far more complicated than any he'd ever experienced with women. His ex-wife had certainly never made him feel this way. Elizabeth had been self-contained, selfish really, a characteristic she never tried to hide and of which Nick had been aware when he married her. It almost helped, because her needs were so clearly defined that little was required of him but his money. He and Elizabeth were similar, in fact. Nick had specific, clearly defined needs, too. There was someone in his bed whenever he wanted, someone to be hostess when he needed one, someone to make decisions about the house. For a while he even tolerated Elizabeth's fleeting affairs.

"Nick,'' Kate said, her eyes still nearly closed, "may I ask you something?''

"Sure.''

"Why did your marriage end?"

Nick looked down at her sharply. Did the woman read minds, as well as everything else?

"You don't have to answer, Nick. I just wondered because—"

"Because?"

Kate shrugged and snuggled closer to him. Suddenly being Mrs. Nick Bannister seemed like a lovely position. Not for her, of course, but for someone. And why would you walk out of that?

Nick looked down at her. And then he settled his head back and closed his eyes. "It ended because it just didn't work out, I guess. I'm not even sure why. I guess deep down we each developed needs that didn't fit easily into the kind of marriage we had. And one thing led to another until we argued more than we talked and we were apart more than together. Once I suggested working on the marriage, but Elizabeth laughed. And then she said something that was probably one of her more perceptive comments."

"Oh?"

"She said, in her perfect finishing-school voice, 'My dear Nick, there are certain things in life that are doomed to failure. Marriage to you is one of them."

Nick laughed softly and Kate heard the sadness in his laughter. She wasn't sure exactly what the sadness was for—the failed marriage or something bigger. She leaned her head back and looked up.

"She was right about that, about marriage and me. But anyway, the next day she was gone. Lawyers sent packers to forward her things, and then they appeared in person to take what Elizabeth felt was her fair share of putting up with me those few years. And that was the last I've seen or heard from Elizabeth."

Nick wondered at his sharing all this with Kate. He hardly ever thought of Elizabeth anymore, and it was odd that being with Kate should make him think of her. The two women were as different as squares and circles. Funny that Kate should make him think or feel anything. Except the truth was she did. She did make him feel.

When the plane finally landed in Kansas City, it was four o'clock in the morning and Nick helped a sleepy Kate from the plane and into the waiting limo. "I'm driving," he said.

"But how will you get home from my place?"

"We'll worry about that when we get there."

When they had pulled up in front of her house, Kate looked up at him. She followed the firm line of his jaw with her eyes and fought against touching it. She swallowed hard.

There was a long silence. The sweet pleasure of being together had moved along with them from the airplane to the limo and now hung there in the air. All around them were the night and the sounds of a sleeping world, but inside the car, the atmosphere was startlingly intense.

Nick reached out and touched her shoulder. He felt the emotion spark through his fingertips and shoot up his arm. He wanted to go to bed with Kate more than anything in the world. It was the only thinkable finale for the remarkable hours they had spent together.

Kate lowered her head, intent for a minute on the plaid fabric of her skirt. She raised her head slowly. "The crazy thing is, I want to sleep with you, Nick. I want to invite you up, I want you in my bed. But those wants I take very seriously, and I can't expect you to share that seriousness."

The words were ones Nick had already played with in his mind. He knew intuitively Kate didn't romp around in men's beds. And he knew even more clearly that Kate was right, that making love meant different things to each of them. He was sure there were things like commitment and relationships and sharing and love coating her idea of intimacy. To him, the perplexing question here was what was attached to *his* idea of it.

Nick nodded. "Yeah, Kate I know. This is the damnedest thing." He slipped his fingers beneath the fall of her hair and rubbed her neck.

A light flickered on in an apartment on the first floor. Kate turned and looked at it. "My landlady," she said.

"I suppose if I don't let you go she may come out after you."

Kate managed a small laugh. "She does look out for me. The neighborhood's not the greatest and Mrs. Fishbein considers herself responsible for the young, defenseless females she rents to."

"Not exactly the words I would use to describe you, Kate."

"Oh, I don't know. Right this minute that's kind of how I feel."

Nick lifted her chin until their eyes met. His voice was gentle. "I don't mean for you to feel that way, Kate. I'm not trying to put a trip on you. Come on, let me walk you to the door."

He didn't kiss her. Instead he steadied himself with a long intake of air and helped Kate out of the car. They walked in silence up to the front door, their fingers twined together.

Over Kate's shoulder, through the smudged windowpane of the first-floor apartment, Nick could see the profile of an old woman with a hooked nose. The curtain parted slightly. Ignoring the audience, Nick kissed Kate then, unable to let her go. He held her tight, covering her lips with his. Her response was instant as he had known it would be. Their tongues wound together in a kind of desperate frustration.

Finally Nick pulled away. "I better leave," he said huskily, "or Mrs. Fishbein is going to have a stroke."

Kate's laughter was shaky. "Yeah." She turned and waved weakly to her landlady. The curtain fell back in place. "Me, too," she added. "The stroke, I mean."

Nick smiled. Then he kissed her once more, light and quick. "Time to go," he said with a catch in his voice, and with short movements, he opened the door for her, then turned quickly and walked back to the car.

The kiss stayed with him all the way home. But what tormented his sleep was not the kiss, not the fact that he had enjoyed himself more than he had imagined possible, not the incredible desire he had had to go to bed with Kate. What tormented him was that he not only wanted to make love to this dark-haired woman, but the startling fact that he wanted to be there with her when he awoke in the morning.

Six

It wasn't until she had stumbled into the shower after a few, fitful hours of sleep that Kate remembered Nick still had her limousine.

She would call him as soon as she got to the office, before Harry got in and found out she had actually let one of their cars disappear for a night. Well, half a night, really. Harry would have a fit, tell her how irresponsible she was and that she had no business running a business. He wouldn't really mean it, of course, but there was no sense in getting his blood in an uproar.

It was only by concentrating on the practical matter of the car that Kate was able to function on a rational level. Otherwise she knew she'd be soaring way above the practical realm of showers and coffee and getting to work. She'd be back in that plane making love to Nick Bannister in the very private shadows of her mind.

Kate breezed through the door to the office a short time later and stopped short just inside the door. Harry was already there, sitting at the desk and drinking coffee. He was smiling, and even though Kate thought it a peculiar kind of smile, it still meant he hadn't found out about the car yet. She breathed a sigh of relief. "Hi," she said, slightly out of breath.

"Hi yourself." Harry looked her up and down. "You look tired."

"Thanks a lot, Harry. What a thing to say, 'You look tired.' Where's 'You look beautiful today, Kate? Ravishing. A breath of fresh air.' "

Harry just sat there, with that odd smile on his lined face.

Kate frowned. "Harry, what's the matter with you?"

"With me? Nothing, at all. Now with you, my little one, that just might be a whole different story." The smile was broader now, stretching all the way from one ear to the other.

"Okay, what's wrong?"

"Nothing. In fact, everything's coming up roses." He laughed out loud as if he had just said something incredibly funny, and he began humming an old tune.

Kate found herself laughing, too, even though she had no idea why.

Finally Harry, still humming, got up and took her by the arm. He steered her down the narrow hallway that led to the garage.

"Where are we going?"

"Got something for you to see."

Kate cringed as he opened the door. But instead of the usual odor of grease and leather polish, she smelled flowers. Roses, to be exact. She took a step past Harry.

There in front of her was her polished and shiny Grand White Knight. And inside of it, filling the seats and the floor and table as well, were enormous bunches of budding yellow roses.

"Oh, my," Kate murmured.

"Oh, my? That's all you can say?" Harry was beside her now.

"Harry, you shouldn't have." She turned and looked at him with a teasing smile.

"I know. So I didn't. But who did? Who filled the Knight with roses, as if you didn't know?"

"He's crazy," Kate murmured. She opened the door and pulled a single rose from one of the bouquets.

"Yep, crazy in love."

"No, Harry. Just crazy extravagant."

"Why did he do this?"

Kate shrugged. She looked over the flowers and spotted a small white card stuck into one bunch on the driver's seat. She pulled it out and read it out loud:

To a lovely lady
in memory of a lovely night
spent soaring above the clouds....

Nick

"I see," said Harry, and he stretched out the two simple words until they dripped with innuendo.

"No, Harry, you don't."

"Then what are we talking about here?"

"We had dinner last night, that's all."

"Some dinner."

"In San Francisco," she added softly.

Kate cradled the phone between her shoulder and ear and leafed through the hospital contract while she waited for someone to answer.

When Nick's voice came over the line she nearly dropped the receiver into her coffee cup. His voice wasn't that unusual, but it was now coated with overtones and feelings. How could that happen so quickly? Kate wondered. It had been a mere three weeks since she had first laid eyes on Nicholas Bannister. Three weeks. A lifetime.

"Hello? Is there anyone there?"

"Nick?" Kate said quickly, extricating herself from those thoughts. "Sorry. I was distracted."

"And now I am. Hearing your voice does that."

Kate felt her cheeks. They were warm. "I called to thank you for the rose garden you planted in the White Knight."

"Well, it was a night for roses."

"It was a wonderful night." Kate paused for a moment and then went on. "How did you know yellow roses were my favorite flower? My father used to bring me one whenever I did anything he thought deserved a rose."

"Like what?"

"Oh, mostly he had to make up things." She laughed, a husky, deep laugh that sprung from a new kind of joy.

"I don't believe it," Nick said. "You probably got them for getting perfect report cards, for helping old ladies across streets, for—"

"Stop," Kate said. "I was never even in Girl Scouts!"

"When can I see you again?"

Kate's laughter died in her throat.

"Kate?"

"This is really ridiculous, you know."

"I know. So when?"

"Friday?"

"Ten minutes from now would be better, but Friday will do. I'll be by about six-thirty."

Kate hung up and sighed softly. Then she leaned her head back against the tall chair and rubbed the soft petals of a perfect yellow rose against her cheek.

On Friday, the new maternity service at St. Joseph's Hospital was launched with fanfare.

Not only were three new mothers and fathers squired home in luxury with their new babies, but one of the mothers happened to be a television anchorwoman and the press had a marvelous time with the story.

Kate was beside herself. The publicity was beyond anything she could have afforded to buy.

When she was asked to be on the evening news that night she and Harry hugged each other crazily.

"Your mom and pop, Katy—they'd be so proud—"

"*Are* proud, Harry. And Mom is restraining Pop right now, telling him he'll burst his buttons."

They hugged again, then Kate tried to settle down and work out a very pressing problem: what would she wear for her first television appearance?

Nick Bannister rushed home from work after signing a new contract that would net his company several million dollars in the coming fiscal year. But all he could think about as he toweled off after a brisk, no-nonsense shower, was Kate Morelli.

He tried hard to remember when he'd been in a woman's company half a dozen times in succession without at least one or two of those times ending up in bed.

He couldn't. In fact, it was difficult to remember being in the same woman's company for that many times in a row.

What the hell was going on? Just that morning he'd received a call from the Richard Chandlers inviting him to fly up to their farm in Connecticut for the weekend. Dick had listed a bunch of other good-time people who would guarantee an incredible weekend. Nick had said no. And then he'd hung up and laughed for no reason.

At exactly six-thirty he arrived at Kate's door. He found her mailbox in the dimly lit entryway and pressed the small button above it.

He didn't have firm plans for the evening. It was seeing Kate that was uppermost in his mind: what they did didn't seem to matter much, which was strange for a man who always had the best theater tickets, reservations for the most desirable table at the best restaurant, and was invited to the choicest R.S.V.P. parties many weeks in advance. He and Kate could sit on a park bench and count stars and it would be okay with him. Maybe they'd see a movie. He hadn't been to a movie in years.

Nick pressed the bell again, wondering if it was broken.

Finally, after drumming it impatiently with his index finger for what seemed an interminably long time, an elderly lady came out. Nick looked at her more closely and recognized her. It was Kate's landlady.

"She's not here," Mrs. Fishbein said to Nick, squinting her eyes to get a clear look at him.

"You're sure?"

"Sure, I'm sure. I'm the landlady here, aren't I? And I know what goes on in my place. Miss Morelli is out for the evening. She left in a fancy car a while ago. So you'd better be off now yourself. Go on—"

Nick scowled. He started to press the woman for details, but decided quickly it was futile. Kate wasn't there. And arguing with the old woman wasn't going to change that. He turned and strode out into the breezy night.

A short while later Nick sat at the bar of Starker's restaurant nursing a Scotch-and-water and analyzing the situation. He shifted on the stool, turning his back to the staircase to avoid seeing anyone he knew.

Nick had never been stood up before. He took a long swallow of Scotch and examined the feeling. It was definitely a mixture, a complicated emotion. There was anger, disappointment and a slight bit of anxiousness thrown in. Closer examination indicated it might be worry. Kate didn't seem the kind of person to go off without a word. He scowled and drummed his fingers. The bartender, obviously recognizing a man who didn't want to talk, refilled his drink silently and drifted off to the other end.

The most irritating thing about the whole damn situation was that it bothered him. Nick didn't like involvements that stirred up emotion. It wasn't the way he ran his life. Maybe he should have gone to Connecticut. He rubbed the back of his neck to ease the tense muscles, and as he lifted his head, his attention was caught by the evening news telecast on a set above the bar. The sound was low to accommodate a piano player on one side of the room, but it wasn't the sound that seized his attention. It was the navy blue wool hat that sat on the news anchor's desk. It looked familiar to him. It was a chauffeur's hat. And when the camera zoomed in on it, Nick knew immediately where he'd seen it before.

"Turn up the television," he called to the bartender.

The young man pushed a button on the remote control and anchorwoman Jessie Peterson's pleasant voice floated across the bar.

"Tonight's spotlight on business is about a special young woman who has done amazing things with a small enterprise," she said.

While Nick watched, the camera pulled away to include the woman at the newscaster's side. "Well, I'll be damned," he said out loud. The bartender responded by pushing a bowl of peanuts in front of him. "You know her?" he asked.

Nick nodded, but his attention was riveted on the woman who was smiling out at him, her face flushed. Her voice excited him more than the business deals that filled his days.

The newscaster asked her to put on the chauffeur's cap, and though Nick knew Kate wouldn't have liked a silly display like that, she did so anyway. She looked beautiful in spite of it, impish and so damn appealing he nearly reached out to the screen.

"Nice-looking woman," the bartender murmured, his eyes filled with more than appreciation. "A chauffeur, they said."

"She's a beautiful woman," Nick said, his eyes glued to the set. She wasn't a chauffeur—she was Kate, a lovely, sensual, desirable woman.

Kate was explaining about the first day of the hospital limo service while the station showed a short video clip of a new family's trip home. Harry, in full uniform, stood proudly beside the car, his lined face bathed in a grin. Even the infant seemed to be smiling as the radiant new mother lifted him into the padded blue car seat. Then the husband held the bottle of champagne up to the camera, and while the world watched and the words *Morelli's Limo Company* seemed to leap from Harry's hat to the top of the screen, the emotional new father toasted his wife and baby, tears of pride streaming down his face.

A gray-haired man sitting next to Nick commented to no one in particular, "There isn't an advertising company worth its salt that isn't eating its heart out right now, wishing they'd put that thing together."

The camera went back to the newscaster who was speculating on the incredible amount of work it must take to put together a program like Kate's special chauffeuring services. It was when she sweetly asked Kate how she had any time for a private life that the look on Kate's face changed. Her smile fell and a startled expression took its place. Then, she sighed, smiled a faded, leftover kind of smile and said, "It's hard to find time. And sometimes my private life even gets forgotten." She looked directly into the camera. "I'm so sorry," she murmured softly.

"Yes," the newscaster said brightly. "And what a fine story it is. I'm sure we'll be hearing more about Kate Morelli and her grand fleet of limos in the days to come. Thank you, Ms. Morelli, for talking to us this evening."

A commercial came on and before the program returned, Nick was in his car heading west toward the television station's offices on Shawnee Mission Parkway.

Kate was just coming out of the building when he pulled up in front of the main entrance. He was out of the car in seconds.

Kate stopped, looked at him and smiled sheepishly. "You saw it—"

Nick didn't say anything. Instead he wrapped her in his arms and kissed her. What began as a simple greeting quickly expanded into a kiss that released all the pent-up emotion that had been plaguing him for hours. Finally he pulled away. "You were great," he said quietly. "It was worthy of a rose, but I didn't have time."

"Only one?"

"Considering the circumstances, yeah. Two at the most. Even though you were the most wonderful thing to happen to the evening news for fifty years, I still got stood up."

"I forgot, Nick. I'm so sorry."

"I know, I heard."

"It slipped out."

"That happens."

"I didn't know if you'd even be watching."

"It was purely by chance."

Kate shook her head. "I don't think so. It was fate. All this is." She looked up at him, her eyes wide and sincere, her face bathed in moonlight. "Did I really do okay, Nick?"

Nick's heart twisted. A huge lump formed in his throat, and he had to look away for a minute. She was doing it again, crawling inside of him, igniting his skin and a whole lot of other things. When she appeared on the news he had been filled with relief, as if he'd found something he'd lost briefly. The urge to see her, to hold her before she disappeared again had propelled him out of the lounge and to the television studio.

"Nick?"

He looked down at her, coughed and said, "I think you missed your career. You should be on television all the time instead of running a limo company. You were great."

"It was all spur of the moment, you know. Otherwise I'd have let you know."

Nick nodded.

"Harry called the studio and said we got calls from a couple of other hospitals, as well as an orphanage that thought it might be a neat idea for kids' birthdays. You know, a limo ride to McDonald's—"

Nick was half listening. He knew she was excited from the rush of being on television. But his own kind of rush, the one creating havoc inside of him, was considerably blurring his concentration.

"So," she was saying, "the night is young. Do we still have a date?"

"I'm here, aren't I? What would you like to do?" Nick hoped she wouldn't throw it back in his court. There was only one thing on his mind right now, and it wasn't a night on the town.

"Well..." One hand pressed against her stomach.

"Ah, the woman has an insatiable appetite." But it couldn't compare to his, Nick thought. No, not in a million years. He took Kate's elbow and headed toward the car. Tonight he would give her food, anything she wanted, the best Kansas City had to offer. And he'd try to drown the desire she lit in him beneath a Kansas City strip steak. Tonight. He hoped Kate wouldn't be hungry when he took her home. But he knew he would be. And he didn't know how much longer he could keep his own appetite in check.

Seven

The next Saturday Kate met Nick at his office as they had decided. He'd take the rest of the day off, he had told her, but he had to put in a couple of hours to keep things running. He had been intrigued when she had insisted on planning the day herself. He had suggested some day trips to her—flying to his lodge in Vail to see the aspen trees, or to Chicago to see the Gauguin exhibit.

But after having been wined and dined and entertained by Nick, Kate was adamant that she have her turn.

"I need to show him *my* world," she had explained to Harry. "He needs to know I'm a simple kid with simple tastes."

"Nothing simple about you, Kate," Harry had said gruffly.

"No, you're wrong and you know it. I don't like all that jet-setting. I'll confess something to you, Harry— I don't even like Nick's house." She said the words in a whisper. "It's all so extravagant. I don't belong there. And when we're surrounded by all those things, I wonder sometimes if Nick really knows me and what I'm all about."

So she'd planned a simple trip that would take one tank of gas, and a dinner that would cost a fraction of what Nick spent daily on flowers. And then he'd see the plainness of her. And then...? And then the ball would be in his court.

Kate sat in the lounge area outside Nick's office suite and waited patiently for Sylvia to finish giving him the messages that had come in the last hour. She looked up and smiled as Sylvia and Nick walked out of the office.

Nick's face broke into a smile when he saw her sitting there and Sylvia smiled, too. Once Nick had told his secretary that Kate was okay, the older woman had broken down and accepted her comings and goings and phone calls without further recriminations.

"Is that it, Sylvia?" Nick asked.

"Yes." Sylvia glanced down at her list. "Oh, one more thing, Mr. Bannister, but it's all rather mysterious. A woman called long-distance asking questions about you. She said she was with some sort of an agency, but the meaning of it all was rather muddled."

"What kind of things did she ask?"

"Odd, things, most of which I wouldn't answer, of course. Were you married and if so to whom, that sort of thing. And then things about the annual report. None of it fit together tightly so I gathered it was some fledgling magazine reporter assigned to do an article on Worldwide Systems and she didn't have much finesse in her approach.''

Nick frowned. ''Do you know where the call was from?''

''Boston.''

Nick stiffened. Boston made him think of Elizabeth, and thinking of Elizabeth always brought that same spurt of anger and failure, anger at the fractured life she'd left him with, and failure that he hadn't been able to make a go at marriage. But connecting Elizabeth to this phone call was absolutely ridiculous. He hadn't heard a word from her in almost three years and she of all people didn't need to call and inquire about his business. She had left with a fair amount of his money and she had always had plenty of her own. The one thing she didn't need was more financial security.

''Well, if it was worth anything,'' Sylvia was saying, ''I'm sure we'll hear from them again.''

Nick nodded. Then he pushed away the disquieting thoughts and turned his total attention to Kate. She had on blue jeans today, worn and fit to her small frame perfectly. A faded green cable-knit sweater matched her eyes and her thick black hair was loose and windblown. She carried a huge lumpy backpack on her shoulders. He knew she probably had given little attention to her looks, but to Nick she was a breath of fresh air, a lovely woman advertising all the things in the world people took for granted such as blue skies and clean air. ''Kate, you look great,'' he said. ''Come on. Let's get out of here.''

''I'd say you're plunging into a day with me quite admirably, Mr. Bannister. No fear?'' Kate said.

"Yeah. Inside I'm quivering like jelly."

"The day won't hurt. That much I'll promise you," Kate said as she took his arm. They walked out to the bank of elevators and were whisked down to Nick's private parking place.

Nick lifted Kate's backpack into the backseat, waited until Kate was settled beside him, and pulled the car out onto the street.

"Where to?" he asked.

"Go west, young man."

"And?"

"And that's all you need to know for now." She grinned, a smug, satisfied grin, and Nick turned the car onto Ward Parkway and headed toward Johnson County and the country beyond. Not being in charge created a peculiar sensation within Nick; it was not the role in which he usually found himself. Once he had figured out his parents years ago, realizing that together or apart they couldn't be counted on, Nick had become an extremely independent person. Whether it was in his personal life or business transactions, he was always in charge.

Letting Kate Morelli lead him around blindly was something new. His initial resistance was instinctive. But now, after Kate had been insistent that this be her day, he was finding it rather enjoyable, something he might even get used to, given the right circumstances.

"Am I dressed okay for this mysterious trip?" Nick asked.

Kate had told him casual clothes and had been curious how Nick would interpret it. He wore a beautiful hand-knit sweater with an Aztec design in deep blue wool that matched his eyes, and a pair of good fitting blue jeans. Flung carelessly over the backseat was a suede jacket that probably cost more than Kate made in a month. She looked at him as he turned the car onto the interstate. "Yes, you're dressed fine. You look great, Nick." An elegant, seductive cowboy, that was what he looked like. She took a deep breath. Well, she had incredible self-control. Harry told her that all the time.

"Hungry?" she asked Nick.

Nick smiled. "Nope." That was a lie. He was hungry for her, with a hunger that grew every time he was with her, and today is seemed especially strong.

"Well, let me know when you are. I brought a Thermos and some sandwiches in my backpack."

The sun beat down on the wide, wavy farm fields on both sides of them and they fell into silence, absorbed in the beauty of the day and the titillating pleasure of each other's presence.

"Some day," Kate said some time later, "I'm going to live in a house that has lots of green like this around it."

"A farm?"

Kate shrugged. "Probably not a farm. But it'll be somewhere where there's room to run and where kids don't have to be quiet because the neighbors are still sleeping." Her voice became more animated as she went deeper into her fantasy, and Nick listened carefully. "It'll be a big white house," she said, "with enough bedrooms for all the kids and a huge back porch for summer suppers and birthday parties." She laughed. "Who knows, maybe I'll even have a swimming pool for the kids. Or a small lake. And at Christmas time we'll string lights along the huge pine trees beside the house and decorate snowmen in the front yard."

"What if there's no snow?"

Kate smiled, her eyes sparkling, and rushed on. "Oh, there'll be snow. And the house will have fireplaces all over the place, big stone or brick fireplaces to warm our toes and fingers after walks in the cold or after the kids have built snow forts out beside the fence."

"Anything else?"

"Uh-huh. Shutters. The house will have forest-green shutters beside the wide windows, and breezy gauze curtains that flap in the wind on summer days."

"Sounds nice."

"It'll be wonderful."

"Is your house out in the country?"

"No, at least not far out. It has to be close enough to town so the ice-cream truck can find it. The kids will save their allowance and run out to the street to buy red and blue pops on sticks."

"Ah," said Nick.

"At night we'll stand outside on the smooth lawn and wait for the dark. And when it finally comes it'll bring fireflies and the kids will grab empty peanut-butter jars and chase the tiny dots of light. Reezers will make lots of noise and—"

"Reezers?"

"Cicadas. My mother always called them reezers because that's the sound they make."

"Oh." Nick had lived in the same city as Kate, was a child just the same as she had been. But somehow he had missed something. He hadn't listened to cicadas, had *never* heard them called reezers, and the thought of catching fireflies in peanut-butter jars with his father was absurd. In fact, peanut-butter jars were absurd. His peanut-butter sandwiches had been made with crustless bread and served by maids and cooks. He had never seen the jars.

The odd thought lingered with him as he listened to Kate go on about her home in the sky. She was looking out the window while she talked, and for a brief moment, Nick wondered about the reality of thoughts. He could hear the reezers and feel the house she talked about, could almost feel its existence as she built it in her mind. He wondered about the man Kate had in mind to live in her green-shuttered house. Before he could ask, Kate began motioning for him to turn off the highway and head west on a two-lane country road.

Nick looked around for familiar highway signs but there weren't any.

"Don't fret, Nick," Kate said, patting his leg. "We're almost there."

"Almost where?"

"Oh, aren't you coy," Kate answered. She laughed and then turned around and got her backpack. "Here, this will keep you from asking too many questions." She pulled out an enormous turkey sandwich, piled high with tomatoes and shredded lettuce and thick slices of Swiss cheese.

Nick took it greedily, one hand still guiding the car expertly along the road. "You thought of everything," he said between bites.

"Tried to," Kate answered, pulling the tab off a can of diet cola. She fiddled with the radio but could only find football games so she turned it off. "The wind can be our music," she said, and turned down the window a crack.

"A perfect traveling sonata," Nick said.

By the time they reached the small sign welcoming them to the tiny town of Council Grove, Kansas, Nick didn't care where they were. An unusual sort of peace had crept into him.

He looked around at the square white houses and neat patches of front lawn. And then he saw the sign declaring Council Grove the recreation center of Kansas. He smiled. "Is this our destination?"

Kate nodded. "Ever been here?" she asked.

"Never."

"Good. Then I can introduce you to something just like you've done for me. My parents and I used to come here a lot. Once a season, at least. We'd fish at the lake not far away, then walk the quiet streets. There's a century-old tavern that makes the best biscuits and pies you've ever tasted in your whole life. Sometimes we went there for Thanksgiving, stuff ourselves with mashed potatoes and turkey and pumpkin pie. It's not at all fancy, Nick. It's a wonderful slow town—"

They passed a brick building with a massive gnarled oak tree hugging its front. "That's the post office," Kate explained. "Before the building was there, the Santa Fe Trail pack trains used to exchange mail in the tree. That very tree, can you imagine?"

Innocent amazement crept into her voice and Nick was hostage to its charm in an instant. He pulled up to the curb and they got out of the car and walked over to the tree. "I used to climb up here," Kate said. "I'd pretend I was waiting for the covered wagons."

Nick watched her eyes as she talked. They sparkled and laughed and dramatized her words. Wonderful eyes, he thought.

Kate grabbed his hand. "Come on. There's lots more things to see."

Nick found himself only too willing to be led. He'd flown over these little one-horse towns in his airplane hundreds of times, and he'd always wondered who lived in them, how they survived, what they did and how they could tolerate such an isolated kind of existence. And here was Kate, bubbling along as if she'd just discovered Walden's Pond.

They walked for hours but it seemed minutes. Nick never looked at his watch, so content was he to let Kate draw him into the history of the little place. She told him wonderful stories of the Osage Indians, the origin of the Santa Fe Trail, and pointed out everything from a pioneer jail to the famous Hermit's Cave. The cave was hidden down a hillside in the midst of dense bushes and trees, and Kate held tightly onto Nick's arm as they climbed down the jagged rocks. She slipped once and Nick pulled her close to his side, wanting to keep her there forever.

Finally as the shadows along a brick-lined street grew long, and Nick claimed they had walked at least two hundred miles, Kate slowed down. "Okay," she said, "now for the big treat."

"Oh?" Nick raised his brows, and the look he gave Kate caused hundreds of tiny goose bumps to pop up along her arms.

The feeling had been there all day, just beneath the surface, and Kate knew Nick was feeling it in his own way. They touched at every turn, small gestures justified by narrow pathways and motioning for the other to look at the colors of a tree or the sunset. The touches lingered after a while, grew more intense, more demanding in the message that passed along the nerves of their bodies.

"Food," Kate said. The word was expelled on a nervous breath. "I made reservations at the Hays House for dinner. You'll love it."

Nick looked down at the top of her head. "I'm sure I will, Kate."

Kate's heart skipped a beat. "Okay. It's back on the main street."

They walked along a residential street, then turned toward the tavern.

"What's that?" Nick asked as they passed a large, freshly painted Victorian-style house with a wide porch that spanned two sides and was dotted with wicker rocking chairs, enormous urns overflowing with brilliant marigolds and comfortable gliders. Several couples sat on the porch, having drinks and watching the sun sink down behind the wooded area across the street.

"It's a bed-and-breakfast," Kate said. "It's a grand place. All the rooms are different. They're filled with high four-poster beds and wonderful antiques."

"Hmm," Nick murmured.

"Come on. The restaurant is just around that corner and down a bit." Nick was still lingering, watching the slow play of life on the porch. His eyes were thoughtful.

Kate watched him for a minute, then took his arm and hurried him down the street.

Dinner was everything Kate had promised, but Nick couldn't concentrate. The pork roast was juicy and perfectly done, the twice-baked potatoes were filled with thick sour cream and fresh herbs, and the apple pie was something only a grandmother could have made.

But Nick barely tasted any of it.

When they finally pushed back their chairs and the smiling, friendly waitress whose name was Bertha brought their check, Nick thought he was going to burst. But it wasn't because he had eaten too much.

Kate had tried for a while to ignore the feelings, to bury them beneath the gravy and homemade bread. But she couldn't. They were there between them, stretched as tightly as Bertha's hair net. This trip wasn't turning into what she had intended it to be at all. Nick was supposed to be faced with her ordinariness, with the simple things that entertained her and made up her past. He was supposed to see that vacations for her meant a car trip to a tiny Kansas town and not a jet ride to Shangri-la. The feelings for him that had been causing havoc inside her were supposed to be on hold for the day, but instead they had tricked her and burgeoned until she thought she was going to explode.

When the walked out of the restaurant and Nick headed back toward the brick-paved street, back toward the wonderful bed-and-breakfast with the wicker furniture and four-poster beds, Kate didn't say a word.

"Nick, this wasn't in the plan," she finally managed to say as they walked up the white steps to the front door.

"I know." Nick almost stopped then, knowing that spending the night with Kate meant many things. It scared him. But Kate Morelli had taken over his life, his thoughts, his sensibilities. For the first time in his memory, he was experiencing feelings so enormous that they controlled him. He needed to love Kate.

Completely. Whatever consequences that brought, he would deal with them.

Kate wandered into a small gift shop while Nick talked to the middle-aged woman behind the old, polished desk.

In minutes they were following the same, gentle-faced lady up the wide, curving steps and into a sweeping room with a four-poster bed and double-hung sash windows that looked down over the street. "I'll be back shortly," the woman said sweetly. She looked at Nick, then added knowingly, "The things you wanted will be just outside your door."

A tip seemed out of place so Nick simply thanked her instead, and when the door closed behind them he took Kate into his arms. "You brought me here, Kate."

"I know," she said softly.

"Scared?"

She nodded against his shoulder. The sting of tears made her close her eyes.

"Mrs. Hansen—the woman from the desk—will be bringing us some things—toothbrushes and the like, a nightgown for you—" He drew Kate over to a velvet love seat in front of the windows. "And if you want, my love, we can sit right here and talk, or read, or listen to music."

His kindness touched her. She wanted him so badly she didn't trust herself to speak, so she only smiled up at him and touched his cheek.

A gentle knock and fading footsteps broke into the moment. Nick walked over and opened the door. He lifted a large wicker basket left on the rug in the hall and carried it to the table near Kate. There was a gown, toiletries, a bottle of sherry and two small crystal glasses. Nick poured them each a glassful. He stood at the window sipping his.

Kate took a small drink and then looked over at Nick.

The only light in the room was a small Tiffany lamp. Its soft multicolored glow lighted Nick's profile, and Kate saw her own desire captured there on his face.

"Nick," she said softly, "won't you sit with me?"

He turned slowly and looked at her with a longing so intense it took Kate's breath away. "It's all up to you now, Kate," he said huskily. "I don't think I dare touch you, because it won't end there, you see."

Kate rose from the small sofa. Before Nick's words had settled between them, she was at his side, her arms wrapped around him. She pressed herself into his body. The desire to be one, to have Nick be a part of her, was overwhelming.

Nick buried his face in her hair.

Slowly they moved by mutual consent over to the side of the mahogany bed. It was a high bed with a colorful quilt. Nick helped Kate onto it almost reverently, then sat next to her and wrapped her gently in his arms. His fingers wove through her hair and he breathed in the wonderful fresh smell of her.

Kate's response to his touch was immediate and as instinctive as breathing. She reached up and caressed his cheek. "How can a touch do that to me?" she murmured. "I feel lit up, high, all those things you read about in books and poems."

"Yeah, I know," Nick said. "I think it's dangerous, whatever it is we have. We ought to keep it secret." He lifted her hair and kissed the tender skin beneath. Kate moaned and Nick could feel her whole body respond. With great reluctance he took her by her shoulders and held her slightly away.

"Kate," he said, "I...I want you to be sure you want this. It has to be right for you."

Kate's head fell back and her eyes closed. When she opened her eyes again there were tears in them and a soft smile so sensual it quickened Nick's heartbeat.

"Nick," she said, "almost nothing in my whole life has ever felt as right as this does, right now, right here, with you."

Eight

Nick's breath caught painfully in his throat.

In the light of the moon, Kate's face was luminous and her moist eyes were filled with desire. For a moment he couldn't think, couldn't act upon the feelings that filled him. He wanted to continue watching her, filling himself with the way she looked.

Kate made the first move. "I can't put my tennis shoes on this beautiful quilt," she whispered.

Nick bent low and removed her shoes. He held one foot gently in his hand and was amazed that it fit there, all of it, in his palm. Waves of pleasure rocked through him.

"Now yours," she said. Nick kicked off his shoes and tugged at his sweater, leaving it in a pile on the floor beside the bed.

Kate placed both hands on the solid wall of his chest. She spread her fingers wide, pressing her palms into his skin. It was solid and warm, and beneath the firmness she could feel the rapid beating of his heart. She'd wanted to touch him like this for so long. Was it years? A lifetime?

"You did it," Nick said with a lopsided smile, and slowly he lifted her arms to pull off the faded green sweater.

When her breasts were finally freed, Nick lay her back against the full pillows and absorbed her with his eyes, his body laced with desire. Her breasts were surprisingly full, with small pink nipples that grew firm beneath his gaze. She had a perfect body, Nick thought, absolutely perfect.

Kate met his eyes and held them.

Her initial embarrassment was gone, and all that was left, glimmering brightly, was a smoldering desire. She lay still, waiting. "I want to look at you," Nick said. "Forever."

"No, not forever," Kate answered, taking his hand and holding it against the flat of her belly. "Looking is only the beginning."

He rubbed the firm flesh and the warmth of her seeped into his hand. Finally, forcing restraints into his fingers, he gently cupped one of her breasts and was pleased at how perfectly it fit into his large palm. He kept his hand there, supporting her flesh for his lips. Slowly, lovingly, he lowered his head and kissed her. Her breasts were sweet and firm, swollen now with her desire. Slowly, confidently, he circled her breast with his tongue until Kate squirmed beneath his touch and her breathing grew shallow.

When he finally pulled away, Kate found the cold space between them unbearable. "Nick," she said, the urgent need of her body evident in her voice, "I do want you. So very much..."

The last words were a whisper, a passionate plea that reached right to Nick's soul and his entire body responded. Fumbling with zippers and snaps, they peeled off their jeans and fell into each other's arms. Nick needed to touch each part of her, to caress her, to press his body against hers until he couldn't tell where one ended and the other began.

"You're beautiful, Nick," Kate said when they moved slightly apart again. Moonlight lit his contours and she greedily devoured his body with her eyes. Her voice was hushed. "I knew you would be beautiful."

"You've been thinking about this, then." His fingers roamed across the rise of her breasts, then down over the firm plane of her belly and across the gentle curve of her hips.

"For a long time. Maybe all my life."

Nick kissed the tender lobe of her ear as his fingers continued to explore every beautiful inch of her. "That's a long time, Katy."

"I feel I've known you that long—a lifetime, Nick." Kate's head fell back at the exquisite pleasure that filled her body. It traveled like a river of warm oil through her arms and her legs, through her belly where his fingers circled and came to rest in a gentle massage. She'd never felt like this before—so completely in tune, so entirely absorbed in someone else's rhythm.

Nick's fingers traveled lower and Kate's body arched at the sensation. "Oh, Nick," she breathed.

"Yeah, it's me," he said, his mouth an inch from her ear. "You're doing peculiar things to me, Kate."

Nick turned slightly on his side and pressed against her.

Kate's breath caught in her throat as she felt the swell of him press into her. "Not...peculiar... at...all..." she said. She reached for him then, her hands groping in the darkness. "Closer."

"Closer?" He looked down into those green eyes and saw the power and beauty of the sea in them. He could see love. He smoothed her damp hair back from her face and kissed her eyes, her nose, then traced her lips with his tongue.

"Closer..." Kate struggled with the single word. She was so completely full of desire, of longing, of delicious, overwhelming sensations, that there wasn't any room left for air or breathing. "Nick...I think I'll die if I don't have you...."

He looked down at her with tender laughter in his eyes. "So happens, my lovely Kate, I have my lifesaving badge." He lifted himself up over her with infinite slowness, not wanting the ebb and flow of pleasure to end.

Then slowly, surely, he entered her.

Passion flooded Kate's face.

"Oh, my darling Kate," Nick murmured. He said the words again, the sound of them matching the pleasure surging up inside of him until Kate's name and the feeling were one and the same thing.

As if from a distance, Kate heard him call out her name. It reached her ears in a cloudy, ethereal way. And then she couldn't hear anymore; all her senses were tied inexplicably to the enormous swell of joy inside of her.

Finally the ecstasy exploded all around her into millions of tiny pieces of joy that cushioned her return to earth and to the immense serenity of Nick Bannister's arms.

When Kate awoke the sun had brightened the faded hues of the quilt. A kaleidoscope of color—golden yellows and greens and patches of cranberry—met the slow pulling-open of her eyes. She closed them again and stretched her arm to the side. Memories of the glorious night began to come to life inside her and she smiled, anticipating the feel of Nick's warm, solid flesh.

The other side of the bed was empty.

Kate sat up, pulling the warm quilt up above her breasts. Sunlight flooded the room. "Ten o'clock, at least," she murmured to the empty room. She hadn't slept this late since adolescence. Ten o'clock, and she didn't know where her friend...her very good friend...her lover...was. There. She'd thought it. Lover. Certainly they'd loved. Enormously. With a passion that had overwhelmed Kate. Funny, she thought, how all of those emotions could be hidden inside someone without that person ever knowing it. "Funny...and wonderful. Very, very wonderful."

Nick walked through the door. "That, my love, is the understatement of the century." He crossed the room in three smooth strides and dropped a bag on the end of the bed. He stood for a moment beside her, and then, with one hand on either side of her hips, he slowly leaned over until his lips met hers.

It was a kiss filled with delicious familiarity. Finally Nick pulled away. He wanted to look at her again, to memorize the sight of her waking up, her body still sleepy and rosy from their lovemaking.

It was a beautiful sight.

Nick had been up since early morning, but he had satisfied himself with watching Kate sleep, bathed in pools of moonlight. He had been entranced and imagined her a goddess emerging from a fog, a woodland creature asleep on the dew of soft grass.

Finally, filled with the scent and sight of her, he'd pulled on a pair of sweats that the proprietress had graciously sent up, and he had jogged through the quiet streets of Council Grove, the brisk morning cold propelling his body, and images of Kate Morelli fueling everything else.

"So, how are things?" Kate said, her voice husky.

Nick nudged her over with his hip and sat beside her. "Things have never been better," he said.

Kate's hair curled around her flushed face, and he brushed it back, then traced the outline of her cheek with his fingers.

"I was thinking..." Kate began.

"Hmm," Nick said.

"About last night..."

"Uh-huh..." Nick moved his fingers down to the smooth edge of her collarbone.

"Nick, it was as if I'd been waiting for that—for you—for a long, long time—"

Nick listened carefully while his fingers continued to explore the lines of her body.

"As if somehow," Kate went on, her breathing growing deeper, "I had known you before—"

"In another life?" Nick smiled. His fingers edged the quilt and then slid beneath it, across the warm skin of Kate's chest.

"Yes," Kate said, and she shivered as his fingers played across her breasts. "Something like that...it was so perfect, so comfortable—"

"Comfortable?" Nick said. There was laughter in his eyes.

"Okay, comfortable's not right. Familiar, maybe. Yes, familiar." Her words came out in spurts, riding the edge of budding desire.

"How familiar?" Nick had pulled back the quilt and as the words left his lips, he bent and used them in other ways. Slowly, gently, he circled the hardening nipple of her breast.

"Oh, Nick," she moaned. "See, that's what I mean—" But suddenly she didn't know what she meant, at all, except that in some inarticulate way, Nick was such a part of her now, he must always have been there. Because how could she have functioned otherwise? There would have been a huge, gaping hole—

And then her thoughts dissolved in a symphony of sensations as Nick shed his clothes and slipped beneath the covers. Her hands eagerly found his shoulders and pulled him close.

This time their lovemaking was different. The urgency of the night before had been replaced by a slow, gentle anticipation of delights already known and laid claim to. But the familiarity only ripened the passion and when they loved, Kate cried out with a joy that would always be new.

Spent, they slept for a few minutes, then woke up a second time to the muted noises of a town going about its usual business.

Kate half listened to the sounds and nuzzled as close as she could to Nick's chest. "I smell something," she said.

Nick opened his eyes. "Sunlight? Love?"

"Roses," she whispered.

"Oh," he said, and together they lifted themselves up, resting on their elbows and looking down the length of the bed.

"Well, whattaya know," Nick said.

Sprinkled across the foot of the bed were dozens of tiny yellow roses.

"Nick, what—"

"Looks like roses."

"But what . . . from where?"

"From the garden of my heart," he said dramatically, and reached down to the floor to push the fallen florist's sack beneath the bed. "When we love, Kate, it rains roses."

"As it should," she murmured, looking into his eyes with a love that she couldn't yet express aloud, but that was swelling inside her to such enormous proportions she was sure Nick would soon be able to see it floating all around her.

They showered and dressed and had homemade sweet rolls on the wide porch. A snappy north wind pushed their bodies together on the swing that hung from the slatted ceiling, and when drops of hot chocolate spilled on Kate's hand, Nick licked them off. A surge of electricity passed from his lips on her hand to her heart, and Kate carefully set her mug on the floor and nuzzled his neck.

"Do you suppose anyone has missed us back home?" Kate murmured.

Nick lifted her chin and showed her how much he cared about being missed. Gently, as the swing moved slowly back and forth, he kissed her again.

"Missed us?" he said afterward, giving casual thought to the question. No, at least *he* wouldn't be missed. Carlton was used to his erratic hours and trips. He'd think Nick had jetted off for an impromptu weekend of skiing in Aspen with his friends. But he'd never in a million years guess that his employer, who owned getaway places in some of the world's most exotic, desirable spots, was sitting on a porch in Council Grove, Kansas.

"Why are you grinning like that?" Kate asked.

"Because of you, my wonderful Kate," was all he said.

An hour later they reluctantly bid farewell to the small town and settled into Nick's car for the trip back to Kansas City.

"I almost hate to go home," Kate whispered, pressing herself against Nick. She wanted to keep him close, to touch him so she would know that this was real, that Nick was real.

Nick looped an arm around her shoulders. "Yeah, I know what you mean." His voice was husky. "I sure as hell didn't expect this to happen, Kate."

Kate didn't ask what *this* was. There wasn't any way to put a label on it all. It was too overwhelming. Kate wasn't even sure herself what *this* was, except that she knew she would never again be the same. She looked up at Nick and felt the instant swell of joy inside her. It was a miraculous thing, she thought, what he could do to her, the way he could make her feel. Miraculous and frightening at the same time. She reached up and touched the two-day-old beard that shadowed his chin. "Nice," she said. "And sexy."

"So that's what this is all about, huh, the beard? Kind of like the story of Samson and what's her name."

"Nope. It's not the beard, Nick. And it's not Delilah. It's simply you. You're what this is all about."

"No, it's not me. It's you and me, Kate." And that was the damnable wonder of it, Nick thought. Kate Morelli, the most unlikely woman this side of Timbuktu had wedged herself right down there inside of him without even trying. Making love to Kate had filled a kind of void inside him that he had managed to ignore for a long time. And she had not only filled it; she had flooded him with pleasure.

The planning instinct in Nick made him wonder briefly what was next, but the way he felt about Kate defied the structure of his calendar and his long-range plans and goals. Kate was separate from everything else, and yet already she had become an integral part of him. Had he ever felt this way before? He looked out over the flat, golden fields and couldn't remember. Kate Morelli was so unique, he was sure there would be no other like her in his life.

Kate watched him as he drove. She saw the play of pleasure flit across his face, saw the muscles of his jaw tense for a moment, then relax again. The beginnings of a smile lifted the corners of his mouth. Kate was able to tumble right into his thoughts because they were hers, as well.

Nick and Kate.

Absurd and wonderful.

Nine

Kate had always thought of autumn as a sad time, a time of goodbyes and finales. Leaves fell, the grass turned brown, and summer warmth gave way to the brash, blustery winds of winter.

But this year everything was different. Autumn was beautiful. No, it was incredible. Actually, Kate thought, it was the most extraordinary season in the past twenty-seven years of her life.

The crispness in the air and the colors of autumn were invigorating and breathtaking, but it was more than that. Kate felt as if her whole life were a palette of brilliant colors. The business was rising out of its doldrums, and the loans, although still slightly formidable, were gradually shrinking. But it wasn't just the business, Kate knew. She, Katherine Alexandra Morelli, was thriving, as well. She told herself the reason she felt this way was the business. And the weather. And the fact that her dog, Ishmael, had finally learned to heel.

But the joy she felt went far beyond that. She knew it, Harry knew it, and her cousins and aunts and uncles knew it when she showed up for Sunday supper at Aunt Sadie and Uncle Morrie's house.

"So," her cousin Maria said before she even got out of her coat, "tell me everything that's happened since we last saw you, and don't leave out a single detail. I'll know it if you do."

Kate laughed and asked Maria how her job was going. Her times with Nick were so private, so special, that sharing them was difficult. It was a dream, a fairy tale, and she was terribly afraid that tampering with it too much might make it pop, like a lovely balloon caught on a tree branch. So she smiled, laughed a lot, and told Maria things about Nick's home and his office and in which restaurants he liked to eat.

But she never mentioned the other things, the special way this enigmatic man made her feel when they were alone, the way he said her name that made her heart skip a beat, the way he looked at her with eyes that were as midnight blue as the sky in the middle of a clear winter night, or about the deep laughter that curled its way right into her heart and made it expand with a rich kind of happiness that she had never felt before.

She didn't tell Maria about the way Nick kissed her so that her whole being filled with hot joy, nor the fact that in the last two weeks she had seen him every single day, even if it were only for ten minutes when his imposing figure would walk into her office to deposit a single rose on her messy desktop. "But what have I done?" she'd ask, a thick blush covering her neck and cheeks. "Brought me joy," he'd say simply, and then he'd kiss her firmly on the lips before dashing back to a business meeting.

"Does this fellow Nick like rigatoni, Katherine?" Aunt Sadie asked. "Maybe you should bring him along to supper so we can meet him." They were finishing up the last few traces of Aunt Sadie's famous pasta dish. Aunt Sadie didn't follow the society pages but even she knew who Nick Bannister was, and Kate knew it worried her. From a distance Nick didn't seem to be the kind of man who would fit easily into the Morelli family, but maybe seeing him up close would ease Sadie's mind and take the worry from her heart. That was why she wanted him to come, Kate knew. "Maybe sometime, Aunt Sadie," she said, and quickly changed the subject.

When she got home that night, Kate ran hot water for a bath, then shed her clothes and lowered herself into her claw-footed bathtub. It was one of the few nights since the trip to Council Grove—"their town," as Nick now called it—that she hadn't seen him. He had a late board meeting and Kate had told him not to come over. She worried sometimes about putting restraints on Nick, about making him feel responsible for her when he shouldn't. Besides, there were no commitments between them yet, no building of the future. So she'd set her chin firm and told him she needed some time to catch up on things and he could use some time, too, she was sure.

So now here she was, alone in her ancient bathtub, missing him terribly.

The steamy water rose up to her chin and it was only after her entire body had finally relaxed that she allowed herself to think. The thought that filled her mind like an exploding land mine was Aunt Sadie's suggestion that she bring Nick to a Sunday-night Morelli supper. What worried her about the invitation wasn't the fact that her romance with Nick was still such a private thing. It was the fact that her relationship with Nick was such a fragile one, one in which they had plumbed each other's souls but made no promises. Its definition was so fuzzy that bringing Nick to a family dinner might go beyond the unspoken boundaries and be an intrusion in their relationship. Having him meet her aunt and uncle and cousins was simply something she hadn't thought about before. And, she had to admit, the reason she hadn't thought about it was because she had been on such a cloud that the real world had almost ceased, for a brief while, to exist.

The bathwater began to cool off and Kate stood and reached for a towel. The real world.... The thought hung in the air of her bedroom while she slipped a nightgown over her head and crawled into bed. That was what was all wrong here. She had let herself plunge into a fairy tale once before and it had nearly destroyed her. The real world served her much better, the real world of her limo company, of Harry, of her aunts and uncles and cousins, of Aunt Sadie's friend's son, John, who always took Kate out when he was home for a visit. That world was real. She pulled up the patchwork quilt that her mother had made for her many years ago when her world was simple and fairy tales were read to her and not lived. With a quivering, soft sigh, she settled back against the plump pillows.

She closed her eyes. But it was already too late to worry about the real world, Kate knew.

It was too late because at some unknown moment during the past few weeks, the fairy-tale world had won out over reality. And Kate Morelli had fallen hopelessly in love with its grand, wonderful knight.

"So, Katy, my girl, another day..."

Kate grinned at Harry and closed the file-cabinet drawer. "And more than just another dollar, Harry. Another new contract today. I can't believe our luck."

"Lucky in love, lucky in life," Harry said.

"I never heard that one before."

"But it's the God's truth."

"Sure, Harry." Kate lowered her head so Harry wouldn't read her face. She couldn't hide anything from him these days. Sometimes she came in in the morning and felt Harry knew exactly what she'd done the night before. "Another contract like this and I can retire, Harry."

"Sounds good to me. My sister in Florida wants me down there more, anyhow. And this damnable Kansas City cold hurts my bones."

"Harry, you can go anytime—"

"I know I can, sweet pea. But no way is old Harry going to leave until you're settled. I promised your pa, Kate."

Kate tried to look angry. "Harry, how much more settled can you see me be? I'm almost twenty-eight years old. The business gets better every day. And once it's a little more solid and the new owner will respect the Morelli name enough to keep it forever on our beautiful cars, I'm going to sell it all, just like Pop was going to do, and I'll move on."

"You'll move on to starting that family you want so badly, Katy. Now that's what an old man like me calls settled—a nice little house with a yard, and—"

"—and a dozen little feet scrambling up the oak trees."

"See, you know what settled means."

"Sure, Harry. And you know my dreams as well as I do. We just have different timetables. Soon, dear Harry, I'll make you a proud, honorary uncle, I promise you." She smiled brightly beneath the sudden contracting of her stomach. It was her dream, one she'd never let go of. But Nick had stepped smack dab into the middle of it, imposing, handsome and out of place. Somehow there had to be a way to make it all fit.

"That's my Kate. And I'll hold you to your promise, you can bet on it. Now, we better get this place closed up."

Kate glanced at her watch. "You're right, Harry. I'm meeting Nick for dinner and—"

"Tonight?" Harry's brows pulled together.

Kate looked at him curiously. For weeks Harry had been pushing the relationship, encouraging her, making her leave early and talking about what a great guy Nick was. His sudden frown was odd. "What's wrong?"

"Katie, tonight's Maria's birthday. Your Aunt Sadie will be expecting you."

"Maria!" Kate clamped her hand across her mouth. "Oh, Harry, how awful of me to forget! Oh, thank you." She threw her arms around him and hugged him close. "What if you hadn't told me, Harry?"

"You would have remembered sooner or later, I guess. But you don't usually forget things like that, Kate."

"I know," she said quietly. "I need a dose of real, Harry."

"Going to Sadie's will do it, Kate. I'm going over after a drink at the Grill. I'll take you."

Kate shook her head. "No. I'll need to pick up a gift. And get hold of Nick. Tell Sadie I might be a little late, would you please, Harry?"

"Will do, Katy. You go, then, be about your business and I'll close up here. Go on now, be off with you." His wrinkled face smiled and he kissed her soundly and pushed her out the door.

Kate drew up her collar around her neck to protect it from the early November cold and headed toward the shops. What a scatterbrain she was. Now she was forgetting the thing that had been most important to her in her whole life—the bit of family she had left. "Kate Morelli," she said, staring into the rearview mirror of the car, "get your act together!"

She ran by the Plaza and stopped at Pierre Deux, Maria's favorite shop, to pick out a birthday present. And out of guilt, she spent far more than she should have, and left with a beautifully wrapped purse made from the country-French fabric that Maria loved so dearly. There. Reality. She'd put it all together.

At home she called Nick and didn't get an answer. "Oh, damn," she said to Ishmael. He thumped his heavy tail in response. "He's already left," Kate said. "Well, we'll have to tell him when he gets here, I guess."

The buzzer near her door rang, announcing Nick's arrival. She rushed over and pressed it to let him in, wondering if she'd ever be able to anticipate his presence with a normal heartbeat. She couldn't imagine.

Nick didn't wait for her hello when she opened the door. Instead, he strode in and wrapped her in his arms. "Hi," he breathed into her neck.

Kate's knees wobbled. "Hi, yourself." She pulled away and smiled up at him.

"I sat in the mayor's office today and thought of you. And then I had an insatiable urge for those Polish sausages you like so much so I had Sylvia buy a bagful, but I was still hungry." He nibbled on the side of her neck. "I guess it wasn't Polish sausage I was hungry for, after all."

"Rigatoni, maybe?" Kate asked, her heart clattering crazily. All he had to do was touch her, just a small flick of his fingers, and everything inside of her lit up. She pressed her legs together fiercely.

"Rigatoni?" Nick repeated.

"Yeah. Maybe you're hungry for rigatoni."

"At the Italian Gardens?"

"No, at Aunt Sadie's." Kate pulled away from him to try to clear her head. What was she saying?

Nick looked down into her eyes. "Something's bothering you, my love."

Kate shook her head. "No. Aunt Sadie asked me once if you'd like to try her rigatoni sometime."

"Oh."

"Do you?"

"Well, when?"

"Now. Tonight." There, she'd done it. He could say no, and that would be that.

Nick shifted from one leg to the other. "Well, okay. Sure." Nick paused. No, he didn't want to go to her Aunt Sadie's for rigatoni. He didn't even know what the stuff was. He wanted to sit and look at her, he wanted to hold her and breathe in the scent of her that filled him with such incredible pleasure. He couldn't seem to get enough of Kate. He had heard Carlton telling the maid yesterday that Nick sang in the shower these days. He never sang unless he was drunk. He was drunk on Kate, that was it.

But Aunt Sadie's?

"You don't have to come," Kate said quickly, "but I have to go. It's Maria's birthday and I forgot about it. I'm really sorry. Maybe I could call you when I get home." She had opened the door and stood leaning against it, waiting for him to pass.

"Do you want me to go?"

Kate shrugged. She looked sad and Nick found that unbearable. "I think Aunt Sadie's rigatoni sounds great," he said. "Let's go."

Kate managed a trip to the bedroom to call ahead. She wanted to make sure everyone adjusted to the idea before she got there, so no one would go crazy on her.

"Hi, Kate," Maria said a short time later as she opened the door to Morrie and Sadie's small frame house. "And you must be the Nick Bannister who is making my favorite cousin such a happy person lately." She not only beamed at Nick, but Kate could almost swear she saw Maria wink. Kate groaned into Nick's back.

Harry was already there and he came to the rescue, pumping Nick's hand warmly. "These Morellis will sweep you off your feet Nick, if you don't be careful, but they mean well." And then he winked.

"Do you all have dirt in your eyes?" Kate wondered aloud.

"What's that, Kate?" Maria asked, eyeing the package Kate held in her hands.

"Happy birthday, that's what's that," she said, flinging her arms around her cousin's shoulders and hugging her warmly. "You don't look a day over twenty-four," she added, smiling fondly at Maria and handing her the gift.

"Yeah," said Uncle Morrie, coming in from the kitchen with a heavy tray of antipasto. "Twenty-five today and still the most beautiful kid on the block." He kissed Kate soundly on the cheek. "And you, Katie, are the prettiest, almost twenty-eight-year-old I know. Look at the two of you, such lucky catches for some lucky men."

Please don't wink, Uncle Morrie, Kate prayed silently.

Morrie turned to Nick and looked up at the tall, cashmere-jacketed man. "So, Nick Bannister, I'm Morrie Morelli. Sit with us." Morrie encouraged the invitation with a gentle push toward a wide, well-broken-in recliner.

Nick sat and Morrie took the chair next to him, settling his wide body comfortably into it. He patted Nick's knee. "We've been wanting to meet you, Nick. Kate doesn't come around so much anymore and I need to know the reason behind this—"

"Uncle Morrie," Kate broke in, "I'm over here every week."

"Shh," Morrie said, quieting her with a flap of his hand.

Nick watched Kate and knew she was trying to get everyone to lay off, that she was embarrassed at all the attention he was getting. He grinned at her, telling her he could handle it, and turned his attention to Uncle

Morrie. He answered his questions, talking about Worldwide Systems' expansion program, explaining what his company wanted to do for Kansas City.

Kate watched and listened as she walked in and out of the kitchen with platters of food in her hands and small kids riding on her back. Nick was being friendly and pleasant and she could tell he liked Uncle Morrie. But beneath it all was a discomfort that she had somehow hoped she wouldn't see, a slight holding back. Well, her family tended to come on like a two-ton truck and she could certainly understand. Nick wasn't used to it, to the open affection, the instant intimacy these people tended to nurture. She relaxed a little when she heard him laughing at one of Morrie's many jokes. It would be all right. This had been the right thing to do. She swerved to avoid her cousin Sheila's three-year-old and announced to anyone who could hear over the din that Aunt Sadie said food was on the table.

She grabbed Nick's arm and led him into the crowded, cheerful dining room.

Nick looked around the table, at the cousins and aunts who had been busy in the kitchen, and at the little ones, four little kids who came up to Nick's knees and whose names melted into a long string of sounds that he knew he'd never remember when it was time to go.

"Hi," one of the kids said to Nick. He leaned his head way back to look up the length of this stranger in their midst.

Nick looked down and Kate watched him carefully. Although she tried not to show it, Sammy was her favorite nephew. He had huge brown eyes and a grin that melted her heart. And he adored Kate. For some insane reason, it was important to her that Nick and this tiny person like each other.

"I'm Thammy," the youngster said, crawling up on the chair next to Nick. His freckles seemed to bounce along his cheeks as he talked.

"I'm Nick," Nick said. Kate waited for more, but Nick didn't say anything else. He smiled at Sammy and looked for a minute as if he wanted to talk to him, but then there was only silence.

"Okay, so let's pray," Kate said, pulling everyone's attention away from the little boy who was now looking at Nick curiously.

Grace was said and food followed, endless dishes that were tastier than any restaurant fare Nick had ever eaten. He complimented Sadie lavishly and proved his sincerity by having seconds of everything. Sadie was enchanted and Kate felt encouraged. Maybe he wasn't as uncomfortable as she thought. Maybe it was just the kids. He wasn't used to them, that was all. But the image of Nick stiffly shaking Sammy's little hand lingered and obscured the enjoyment of Aunt Sadie's rigatoni.

After dinner more tiny cousins crowded around Nick's knees, seeking attention from the guest. Sammy's baby sister, Anne Marie, crawled up in his lap, leaned her head against his chest and stuck her thumb in her mouth. When the baby's mother asked if she should take her, Nick smiled politely and suggested Anne Marie would probably be more comfortable on a softer body. The baby immediately sought out Kate, who scooped her up and kissed the pudgy, pink cheeks.

When Kate suggested a short time later that they leave, Nick didn't argue. He knew Kate would have enjoyed staying longer, but he had to get out of there. He felt disoriented, out of place. Kate's family was friendly and warm and funny. But the emotion, the constant reaching out and touching and pulling him into their conversation and their lives, unnerved him. And the little kids reminded him that he didn't know the first thing about them, that he definitely wasn't father material, and that children, Kate's *own* children, were an enormous part of her future.

When Nick didn't call the next day, Kate tried not to worry. She had usurped so much of his time these days she sometimes wondered how his business was surviving. He probably had a million things to catch up on.

Tuesday brought a flurry of snow, but no phone call from Nick. Kate left a message with Sylvia, who explained kindly that Mr. Bannister was in a series of meetings—he had business associates in from the East Coast—as well as some personal things to take care of, but she was sure he would call just as soon as he had a free minute.

That night Harry insisted Kate join him for a sandwich before she went home. He was getting too skinny and he couldn't stand the look on her face. Bad for business, he said.

Kate nodded numbly. She still believed she'd hear from Nick. He simply wouldn't drop out of her life this way. Not the Nick she loved so desperately.

They stopped at Houlihan's in the Plaza for a bowl of onion soup and a hamburger. The bar was packed with happy people and Kate was thankful for the noise. It helped put her thoughts on hold.

After they ate, Harry suggested a walk around to help digest the food. Kate knew he was babying her and she gave in to it gratefully. She linked her arm through his, forced a smile on her face and chatted with him about limos and leather upholstery cleaner and spark plugs, about everything but Nick.

As the approached Starker's restaurant Kate felt a sad lump form in her chest. She remembered that night eons ago when she had dragged Nick there to convince him the Morelli Limo Company was wonderful, and had come away thinking Nick was wonderful. A wonderful knight, a handsome rogue.

She stood silently for a minute while Harry commented on the horse and carriage plodding by. The horse walked just like him, Harry was saying, but Kate barely heard. The restaurant was crowded as always, with people coming and going and stopping on the curbside to chat. A group of well-dressed people rounded the corner and walked toward the door. In the center was a tall, regally dressed woman, her long body fully and gracefully cloaked in an elegant fur. She laughed at something the man next to her said, then tucked her arm in his and walked through the door.

Kate's heart stopped. It was Nick. No question about it. Tall and imposing and dressed to the nines, as Harry would say. Her Nick. "Personal things to take care of." Sylvia had said.

With a heart so heavy she wondered how she was able to walk, Kate turned and walked quietly back to the car.

Kate slept that night in starts and stops, her mind jostled by disturbing and sad images. And in between, squeezed as tightly in place as a cornerstone, was the hope that tomorrow she would see Nick, tomorrow she would talk to him, hold him close, and everything would be all right. Hours later, when angry voices crept into her foggy consciousness, she thought it was another dream, another image to block out, another hurdle to overcome before morning would rescue her.

But the voices continued and eventually she pulled her eyes open. The sounds were still there, invading the small room through the one partially opened window. Kate dragged herself out of bed to see if anyone needed help. Every now and then there were problems in the neighborhood. A bud of fear opened up inside her.

A freezing gust of wind assaulted Kate as she opened the window wider. Familiar voices rose up on the cold air. She heard Mrs. Fishbein, her landlady, first, protesting angrily that no decent person visited anyone at one-thirty in the morning. And then she heard the voice that sent half her body hanging out the window into the chilly air. Nick. It was Nick arguing with Mrs. Fishbein, insisting that the landlady let him inside so he could ring Kate's apartment.

"Nick," she called out to him, her hair whipping wildly about her face, her heart wedged up in her throat.

Nick stood back and looked up. "Kate, I love you."

"Oh, Nick," Kate said. "Nick, I love you, too."

"And I love to sleep!" yelled Mrs. Fishbein.

Another window opened nearby and a sleepy voice yelled out, "Then let him up, already!"

"It's okay, Mrs. Fishbein," Kate mumbled. "You can let him in."

Kate could hear the door being unlocked, and then she opened her apartment door and listened to Nick's footsteps getting louder and louder as he came closer to her. She met him on the landing, her flannel nightgown flapping loosely about her shaking body.

Nick scooped her up and carried her inside. He kissed her hair, her neck, her lips.

"I've missed you, Nick," she said softly.

Nick carried her over to the couch and set her down next to him. He didn't remove his jacket, he just sat there holding her in his arms in a drafty apartment, a welcome warmth finally returning to his heart.

"Kate," he said finally, gently brushing her hair off her face, "I'm sorry I haven't called."

"It was Morrie and Sadie's. It was too much for you, all that family."

"No, Kate. Well, yes, in a way, it was. But only partially. The past few days have been frantic at work. And my sister, Sharon, called to tell me she was getting married again."

His sister. Something personal, Sylvia had said . . . "Oh," Kate said softly.

"Yeah. Some guy she met in the Alps a couple of weeks ago. She barely knows his last name. And, as usual, Sharon needed some money fast so I had to sell some stocks of hers. And then there was a company merger. I had a couple here from New York who wanted to sell their family firm. The woman was a real barracuda, but after a meal at Starker's tonight they both mellowed."

Kate smiled as the memory of the lady in the fur coat floated out the window.

"And some law firm in Boston has been leaving cryptic messages—"

"It's okay, Nick. I understand."

"No, Kate. Don't be so understanding. I still should have called. I don't know, after your cousin's birthday—seeing you like that in the middle of a family and loving all those kids—I thought maybe you needed some space, some time to get a perspective on all this. We both needed it. But I missed you like crazy, Kate." His fingers played with her hair. "I thought about you all the time."

Kate felt the sting of tears behind her lids.

"I don't know exactly what to do, Kate, and I'm not usually in that predicament. We're so different, our lives, our expectations."

"But something's the same. This feeling, Nick, it overwhelms me. I'm different because of you, fuller, richer."

"I know. I didn't know what it was to really love someone before. I do love you Kate. I'm not sure of a whole lot else, but I do love you. Enormously. And tonight, after I got back to the house, I knew I couldn't wait anymore. I had to tell you. I don't know what will happen, where it will go, but I do know this much, that you've become a part of my life and it— I will never be quite the same again."

Kate wound her arms around his waist and held him tightly. She didn't know what would happen, either, and that fact frightened her more than she would ever admit to Nick. But for now, for this one moment, maybe their love was enough. It was so huge. She took in a long, steadying breath.

Yes, for tonight surely that would be enough.

Ten

The acknowledgment of Kate and Nick's love was a freeing thing for Kate. She now felt her smile and joyous disposition could be flung across the whole world. There was no reason to keep it secret any longer, because she loved Nick and he loved her back. But at the same time, the future loomed out long and winding and complicated in front of her, and she found it difficult at times to be content with the joy Nick brought her each day. She wanted their present to build toward a future. Together.

But those thoughts were kept secret, locked tightly away inside her. One day everything would all fall into place, she told herself. One day, their enormous love would simply propel them into the next chapter, the next step of their life. Together. Surely it must be together.

Kate found Nick's love did something else for her: she no longer felt uncomfortable when they were out together and ran into his friends, or when she attended a business dinner with him and sat next to other leaders of Kansas City's civic scene. Nick loved her and that was all that mattered; she could be herself because that was what he loved. And Kansas City society reacted nicely to Kate's openness and confidence. Soon Nick's friends found excuses to sit next to her at the often boring affairs, because Kate always had funny stories to tell about the limo business and the things that transpired on a trip from a hotel to the convention site, or on prom night or when some East Coast mogul came to town and asked if Kansas had trees and running water.

Life was a lovely, joyous whirlwind.

One crisp November night there were no meetings, no plans, no obligations, and Kate suggested taking in a movie at one of the dollar theaters.

"I've never heard of dollar theaters," Nick answered.

Kate laughed and tucked her arm in his. "Your education has been sorely neglected, young man. Come with me."

They went south, out State Line Road to a small shopping center called Watts Mill and bought tickets to whatever movie started next.

They sat toward the back with a huge cardboard container of popcorn between them and Nick slipped his arm around her shoulders. "Hmm," he said into her ear. "I haven't done this since I was fifteen."

"Seen a movie?"

"Necked in one." He nibbled her ear.

"Nick, necking went out with the sixties," she whispered.

"We'll see about that."

"Shh," a couple in front of them scolded, and Kate, red-faced, slipped a handful of popcorn into Nick's mouth to quiet him. He caught the tip of her finger between his teeth and she squirmed in the chair. They should have rented a video, she knew it. It was bad enough keeping her feelings under control in well-lit public places, but the deep shadows of the movie theater might just be more that Kate could handle. Nick didn't even need to touch her these days to awaken her senses; just his presence, or the thought of him while she did paperwork, tore the humdrum out of her day and filled it, instead, with incredible sensations.

The movie played on and Kate and Nick fell into silence; Kate tried to concentrate on the flickering images across the screen. The movie was all about parenthood. There were kids in the movie, lots of them, little ones, big ones. There was laughter, and tears. She looked over at Nick. He was watching it now, too, his face expressionless.

When the movie finally ended with the birth of a baby, Kate's eyes were filled with sentimental tears and there was a lump in her throat too big to talk around. Silently, pensively, she followed Nick out of the theater.

"Nice movie," he said as they climbed into the car.

Kate nodded.

He drove up State Line Road. "The lead guy was funny," he said a short while later when he pulled up in front of her apartment. "A good actor, too."

Kate nodded.

The movie still consumed her. The kids, the laughter and tears, the trials and joys of parenthood, but most of all the birth of the baby. It as almost painful, the sensations that swept through her as she thought about the tiny infant cradled in the mother's arms.

She and Nick walked quietly upstairs to her apartment and she automatically put a kettle on to boil for tea, then poured Nick some Scotch she kept in the cupboard just for him.

"Kate," he came up behind her, wrapping his arms around her waist, "I think we should find you another apartment."

Her thoughts were still on babies and families, on being a mother and a wife, on her dreams.

"Apartment? What are you talking about?" she said, an edge to her voice.

Nick didn't seem to notice the edge. "Apartment. This place has terrible heat, the neighborhood isn't the greatest, the paint is peeling, only part of the stove works. Let me do it for you, Kate."

An irrational anger shot through her out of nowhere. And only much later, after she had told Nick she was exhausted and had to get some sleep, after she had ushered him out of her apartment with only a perfunctory kiss, and after she had stood for a long time at the window in her bedroom staring into the night, did the anger fade away and understanding seep in.

She didn't want a new apartment. What she wanted more than anything in the world was to marry Nick. She wanted to live with him, to love him, and she wanted desperately to have his babies.

* * *

"Why so sad-looking, little one?" Harry asked. "It's been a long time since I've seen those beautiful lips tilted down. What gives?"

Kate forced a smile. "Nothing. Just lots to do."

Harry came over and sat in front of the desk. "You can't fool an old fool, Katy."

Kate forced back the sudden sting of tears.

"Nick?"

She nodded.

"Problems?"

"I love him, Harry," she whispered.

"I know, dumplin'. I sure know that. Everyone knows that who's been within a hundred feet of you. And Nick's just as bad as you are, if not worse. Look at that." He waved his hand at a bouquet of yellow roses that had arrived minutes before, along with a box of cigars for Harry. Then he took her hands and covered them with his wrinkled palms. "And I think it's pretty damn nice, if you don't mind my saying so."

"If only we wanted the same things, Harry."

"Sometimes that takes time, little one. Patience."

Kate nodded.

"Nick's older, had more time to settle into his way. Give him some time, Katy."

"You're right, Harry." Of course Harry was right. How could she expect so much in such a short time? She wasn't being fair to Nick. Their love needed time to deepen, if that was possible, to age, to become richer. And then it would all work out.

She stuck that thought up in the very front of her mind and checked into it constantly the rest of the morning, and when Harry asked her to drive the limo for him because he had to go to the dentist, she agreed happily. She needed to move about, to clear her thoughts, to do as Harry said and not be blinded to the forest because of all the trees, whatever that meant.

Her heartbeat speeded up when the address Harry handed her took her to the Bannister Building. Maybe she'd see Nick, sneak into a quiet corner with him for a minute or two.

But the doorman walked out to the limo immediately when she pulled up, and he opened the car door for a handsome, distinguished-looking gray-haired couple. Kate smiled when they were seated and went to close the partition window, but the man stopped her, suggesting that maybe she could tell them something about the city.

"We've been here before," his wife explained, "but it seems we're always so rushed and today we actually have some extra time before our plane leaves."

So Kate drove them slowly through the Plaza, then around Loose Park and on into Mission Hills and past the gorgeous homes that commanded acres of well-tended yards on winding, hilly streets.

The couple was from California, they said.

"And you're here on business?"

"Yes, at Worldwide Systems."

"Good company," Kate said, her heart galloping as her thoughts turned to Nick.

"Excellent company," the man said, "And let me tell you it's all because of that young Nick Bannister."

Kate's heart skipped two beats.

"I've known him since he was a little tyke. He's certainly nothing like his father."

"You know Nick . . . and his father?" Kate asked, trying to keep her voice steady.

"Yes. Went to school with Big Nick. He was a sharp business man in some ways but—"

"But certainly a terrible family man," the woman cut in.

The two then engaged in conversation with each other, almost forgetting Kate was there as they speculated on Nick's success, commenting on what a miracle it was that he had grown into such a decent person considering his lack of good family life.

"You know," the wife said to her husband, "I remember one year when we were all in Hawaii at a convention and the comment was made that Nicholas hadn't seen his children in over fourteen months. Nicholas had laughed, admitted it, almost been proud of it, or so it seemed to me. He used boarding schools, summer camps, anything to keep those two children out of his hair."

"But . . . his mother," Kate said slowly.

"There were a parade of those. I think Nicholas was married what? Maybe six times?"

"Divorces right and left." "Nannies . . ." "Selfish life . . ." "Kids were a mistake, an accident . . ."

Snatches of Nick's childhood flew through the opening in the car and Kate warded them off, concentrating intently on the road. She knew, of course, that Nick hadn't had a good relationship with his father; he had told her as much. But she hadn't realized how bad it had been because it was so foreign to her to think of a family without love. She shuddered.

And later that night when Nick stopped by to say good-night, she held him tenderly, and then she loved him fiercely with her whole heart and soul.

"Aspen, Colorado . . ." Kate's voice drew out the words until they stretched clear across the car. "I can't believe I'm doing this, Nick. I mean, I don't ski. I don't—"

"You'll ski. You'll be a natural at it."

"How do you know?"

"I know your body, and I know skiing, that's how."

Kate blushed furiously. "Seriously, Nick."

"Seriously, Kate, you'll either love it or you won't. And if you don't, there's a great hot tub out on the deck. It's not that cold yet—you'll probably get a tan. Just relax."

"A hot tub for three days? I'll get all puckered."

"Then I'd smooth you out." He stopped at a light, pulled her close to him and kissed her.

But Kate couldn't relax, even beneath his gentle teasing and the luxurious warmth of his kiss. There was something too decadent about it all. It was a busy weekend for the limo company and here she was flitting off to Colorado and saddling Harry with the whole thing.

"That's just an excuse, you know," Nick said, "thinking the limo company needs you. Harry can handle it just fine."

"Stop reading my mind, Bannister. It's private."

"You're transparent, Kate." Nick squeezed her knee. "But that's just one of the many things I love about you. Now calm down because here we are."

Kate looked up as they drove into the municipal airport and over to the familiar hangar where Worldwide Systems kept its planes. The same young blond fellow she had seen when they went to California greeted them with a friendly wave. "Everything's ready to go, Mr. Bannister," he said as they stepped from the car.

"Great," Nick responded. "All we need to do is throw those bags in the back—"

Just then the door to the hanger flew open and a mechanic rushed out, racing toward them. "Mr. Bannister, you had a phone message. It's an emergency."

Nick drew his brows together. "Emergency? I told Sylvia to handle anything th—"

"It was someone named Carl Tongue."

"Carlton . . . what did he say?"

"Only that there was an emergency at the house. Your house. And that you had to go there immediately. Said it was a matter of 'utmost importance,' that you shouldn't even get out of the car. And then he hung up."

Nick looked at Kate. "Listen Kate, I'm sure it's nothing but—"

Kate was already getting back in the car. "It's okay, Nick. Hurry."

Nick spun the car around and headed back toward home, out of the airport, across the bridge and through the city at record speed. "Damn," he muttered half to himself, "I just took the car phone in for repairs. Maybe I should have called Carlton from the airport. This doesn't make any sense. Nothing is ever an emergency for Carlton. The man could handle a world war single-handedly."

"He must have had good reasons," Kate said softly, her hand on Nick's thigh. An intense fear gripped her heart, but she tried to hide it beneath the calmness. Emergencies for Kate meant terrible things. Emergencies meant accidents; sometimes they even meant death. Nick's frame of reference was different and Kate was grateful for that; at least he didn't have to make the drive with fear in his heart.

They reached the Bannister home in record time and Kate flew out of the car, reaching the front door with Nick only a second behind her.

The door opened before they had a chance to touch it.

Nick and Kate stopped in their tracks, frozen at the threshold.

Standing in the center of the wide foyer, his face as pale as a first snowfall and his stolid demeanor in severe jeopardy, was Carlton. And tangled in his arms, wiggling like a new puppy, was a beautiful, curly-haired little girl.

Eleven

"Carlton," Kate said in awe.

"Carlton!" Nick barked.

"Sir," Carlton said.

The child twisted her head to look at the intruders. Her eyes were huge-round, blue eyes that completely, immediately mesmerized Kate. They were a familiar blue, a beautiful, deep midnight blue. "Oh, Carlton," Kate said again, her eyes never leaving the baby, "Who is she?"

"Shelby is her name, ma'am."

"Shelby..." Kate walked toward the tiny girl and held out her arms. Short pudgy hands reached for her immediately and as Carlton was being relieved of his burden, he breathed an audible sigh of relief.

"Carlton, what the hell is going on here?" Nick was scowling. His eyes no longer looked at the child, but

at the situation. Carlton had called him back from a
wonderful trip with Kate because of a small child he
was having a problem with. This didn't make sense.
He tried to be calm. Carlton was a good man; he
didn't usually act irrationally. "Can you explain why
you called me back, Carlton?"

"Yes. I called you back because of Shelby, sir."

"Yes, Carlton," Nick said, forcing patience into his
voice. "What about the child? Is there trouble you
need my help with? Is she a relative of yours?"

"She's your daughter, sir."

Silence filled the room. It was at once frightening
and stifling in its intensity.

Kate, who had been busy murmuring comforting
things to the bright-eyed child, jerked her head up. She
stopped breathing.

"Carlton, don't be ridiculous," Nick said, regain-
ing his composure.

"No, sir, I wouldn't be that." Carlton walked over
to the hall table and lifted up a packet of legal-looking
papers. He held them in his hand, then looked back at
Nick and said quietly, "I think, sir, we'd better sit
down. And perhaps a glass of sherry wouldn't be out
of order."

An hour later they were still sitting in the den. The
baby had been handed over to Christina, the maid,
who was playing with her in the kitchen. Nick held his
head in his hands, trying to make sense of the information Carlton had laid out in front of him.

Elizabeth had had a child, never told him, never
wanted the contact that that knowledge might bring.
And then she had died of an unforgiving cancer that
had swept through her like a gale wind. Her father, the

only family she had left, was in a nursing home, so she had set legal wheels in motion that would bring Shelby to her father's doorstep.

"Surely I would have known if I'd had a daughter. Surely someone would have contacted me when the child was born...or when Elizabeth became ill. Surely then."

"The lawyer will be back tomorrow to explain it all in more detail," Carlton said slowly. "But it seems Miss Elizabeth's desire was that you be checked out thoroughly, to make sure Shelby would have sound care. That wasn't completed until after she...passed away. And then a telegram was sent." Here Carlton paused, slightly embarrassed. "The telegram announcing Shelby's arrival was thrown out when the new maid—she's no longer with us, sir—spilled tea on it. It was an unfortunate accident."

"This whole damn thing's an unfortunate accident!"

Kate looked up at the grief in Nick's voice. No, it wasn't so much grief as anger. Her eyes widened.

"I can't have a child." Nick looked at Kate as if she could change it. "Kate, this is crazy. I'll have to take care of it." His mind seemed to be drifting off.

"Take care of it?" Kate said. "You mean take care of Shelby. She's not an it, Nick. She's a beautiful little girl. And yes, of course, you'll have to take care of her." Kate had all she could do to remain in the room. She wanted to go to the child, wrap the small girl in her arms and comfort her. But she knew Nick needed her with him. She had never seen him overwhelmed by anything, but he seemed totally at a loss now.

"No," Nick said calmly, turning away from Kate and staring at the papers lying on his desk. "I don't mean take care of Shelby. I don't know the first damn thing about taking care of a child. I mean taking care of the situation. I'll have to do something about the situation." He stood and walked slowly back and forth in front of the fireplace.

Kate stared at him. She wasn't sure what he meant, but a cold chill began to move slowly through her body. When it got to her heart, she silently stood and left the room.

She found Shelby in the kitchen, toddling around the chairs, picking up tiny pieces of cookie that Christina had placed on each seat to entertain her. Soft dark brown wisps of hair curled around her fat cheeks. She was one of the most beautiful little girls Kate had ever seen.

When the tiny child noticed Kate standing in the doorway, she broke into a grin and little bits of cookie fell from her mouth.

Kate's heart melted. She walked over and scooped her up. "Hi, Shelby," she said. "Are you having fun with Christina?"

"Mama?" Shelby said softly, her eyes large and questioning.

Kate hugged her close and kissed the side of her hair. "Mama's not here, sweetie. But it'll be okay. You'll be fine, Shelby." She nuzzled the baby's neck to hide the tears that pressed behind her lids. Shelby smelled wonderfully of powder and lotion—sweet, wonderful baby smells.

She carried the baby into the den. "Carlton," she said, "were any clothes or baby things left with Shelby?"

"Oh, yes, miss!" Carlton stood immediately, grateful to be excused from Nick's presence for a few minutes. Kate followed him upstairs to the guest room, and he pointed to a half-dozen suitcases lined up against the wall. "All that came with the child, Miss Morelli."

"Please call me Kate, Carlton. I think this situation calls for less formality, don't you?"

Carlton smiled at her, the warmest expression Kate had seen cross his face. "Yes, miss...Kate. And if I might say so, I'm terribly glad you're here."

Kate smiled in understanding, then set to work finding diapers in the stash of baby things that had been left to Nick Bannister along with an enchanting little girl.

Kate sat in the Morelli Limo company office the next morning and talked to Harry nonstop, repeating the whole, unbelievable story of Nick Bannister's daughter. "Oh, Harry, you'll melt when you see her. She's the loveliest child in the world."

Harry shook his head. "I don't believe it. Nick must be flabbergasted."

"More than that, Harry. He's in shock." Her voice dropped and her face grew pensive.

"What is it, Kate?"

Kate shook her head. "I don't know Harry. I'm terribly frightened and I don't know why. Nick was...I don't know, different somehow."

"Katy, this is a terrible shock to a man, to find out there's a child of his in the world that he didn't even know existed."

"How would you react, Harry?"

Harry shrugged his shoulders. "Hell, I don't know. I'd probably down a couple jiggers of bourbon, then start worrying about her first date and her college education."

"While you bounced her on your knee, right?"

Harry's face softened. "Of course. I'm a sucker for big eyes and curls, you know that. How old is the tyke?"

"I think around thirty months or so. Harry, when I left there, Nick still hadn't touched Shelby. I fed her, put her to bed, even slept in the room with her in case she was frightened. But Nick never held her, not once."

"That'll change." Harry laughed and lit up a cigar.

"I don't know, Harry. He was all business. He seemed to be looking upon the whole thing as he would a negotiable business transaction."

"Hey, he's a good man, Kate. He'll work it out in his way. Maybe that's how Nick handles crises."

Kate shivered, even though the heat was on and she wore a thick sweater. "Oh, I hope so, Harry, I hope that's all it is. I finally left this morning thinking maybe he would take over, see how lovable Shelby is, how special."

Nick called her several hours later. His voice was tired and worn. "Kate, I won't be able to take you out tonight," he began.

"Nick, of course you won't! Don't you think I know that? Good grief." Her heart soared with love for him. He *was* facing it, fatherhood, having a child. How could she have doubted it? "How is Shelby? I thought I'd come over and help—"

"I don't want to saddle you with that, Kate. Christina's taking care of her while Sylvia's looking for a nanny. The lawyers are coming over shortly to discuss the...situation."

"Oh."

"I'll call you later," he said in a preoccupied tone of voice, and hung up.

A couple of hours was all Kate could take. She couldn't stay away. All she could think about was Shelby. She couldn't think beyond it, couldn't consider what this meant in her life. Her thoughts were completely focused on the small child who had so recently been left without a mother.

Carlton answered the door on her first ring. He looked drawn but greatly relieved when he saw Kate. "Thank heavens, miss Kate. Thank goodness you're here."

"I thought...I thought maybe I could help, Carlton."

"If you hadn't come I might have called the National Guard," Carlton said with a small smile. "Mr. Bannister is in his office."

In the background Kate heard Shelby crying. It was a pathetic sound, broken only by tiny, frantic hiccups. Kate rushed toward the noise. She found a distraught Christina pacing back and forth in the den with the child held tightly against her shoulder. "She won't stop," she said to Kate over the din of Shelby's cries.

"I'll take her," Kate said, and wrapped the shaking child in her arms. "Shelby, it's okay," she soothed, patting her gently on her back. "Kate's here, Shelby."

Finally the cries calmed down and Shelby's little body relaxed in Kate's arms. Christina sat nervously on the edge of a chair. "I don't know much about little ones, miss."

"It's okay," Kate said. "You were doing fine. She's just disoriented, that's all. I'll take over now if you want to go."

Christina jumped up. "I could make the beds, maybe." And she was off before Kate could change her mind.

Kate sat Shelby on her lap and felt the damp, silky strands of her curls. "Oh, Shelby," she said, "what a lovely little girl you are." Shelby responded to the gentleness in Kate's voice and made small sounds in return as she reached up to touch Kate's chin. Small, fat fingers traveled across Kate's face, and she laughed as Shelby found the hoop of her earring and tugged on it. "Nope, Shelby," she said, capturing the small hands and clapping them together. "Not a good toy, sweetie. We'll find you something else."

"Toy?" Shelby repeated. "Good toy."

Kate carried Shelby over to the bookcases behind Nick's desk and searched the shelves. There wasn't much there for a child. That would have to change, just one of the many changes Nick would have to make. But he would. Once he let this little girl into his heart, he'd do anything for her, Kate was sure.

Her attention shifted from the shelves filled with expensive collectibles and books to Nick's desktop. A coffee cup half-filled with cold, stale coffee was on it.

Nick must have sat here last night or early this morn-ing, she mused, thoughts of him filling her heart. "You have a wonderful daddy, Shelby," she said. "You might have to be patient with him, but he'll come around."

"Daddy," said Shelby, trying out the new word.

"That's right, sweetheart, daddy," Kate said, and her heart swelled with emotion.

Shelby responded to the conversation by grabbing a sheet of paper upon which Nick had been jotting notes. Kate laughed and pulled it free of her fingers, then smoothed it out on the green desk blotter. The words *Baby Girl* caught her eye.

Beneath the words was a list. Her eyes scanned the sentences fragments:

Call company attorney
Contact family attorney
Sharon—Hotel Aigle Noir 8888-6489
Cy Rosen, attorney—private adoptions

A lump began to form in Kate's stomach and in-stinctively she hugged Shelby closer to her. She read the list a second time, and then a third. It didn't make sense. Shelby didn't need agencies or lawyers. Shelby needed love.

Sharon...that was his sister's name, the one who recently got married for the umpteenth time. Why was he calling her?

What was Nick doing with this list? The lump grew, a cold, painful presence in the center of her. She looked down at the little girl. Shelby had cuddled against Kate's chest, her thumb stuck tightly in her mouth. Her eyes were half closed and her body was becoming limp with drowsiness.

Kate's heart swelled and she kissed Shelby on the forehead. The little girl's skin was soft and warm. "Sleepy, my darling?" Kate asked, then carefully, without making a sound, she carried the now-peaceful child up to the guest room and gently tucked her into the makeshift crib she had fashioned out of bolsters and chairs the night before.

Three hours later, when Nick returned, Shelby was still sound asleep.

"Kate!" he said, when he saw her sitting in the den. His heart soared. Kate was what he needed right now—a light in the dark, discomforting sea. He'd slept only briefly the night before, and the morning had been filled with difficult phone calls, meetings, lawyers and painful decisions that had to be made about the child. He felt hollowed out, disoriented and needed the grounding of Kate's love. She was the only sane, comforting thing in his life right now. He needed her desperately.

He strode across the room and sat beside her, wrapping her in his arms. "Kate, you're exactly what the doctor ordered."

Kate breathed in the warmth and smell of the man she loved. His arms comforted her enormously, made her feel safe and secure. Slowly her fears melted beneath his love.

"You must be exhausted, Nick," she said against his chest. "These past two days have been overwhelming, I know." She looked up at the strong chin, at the shadow of his beard, and smiled softly. "But

Nick, it will be okay. She's perfect, darling. She's so lovely, and she looks like you, your eyes—''

Kate could feel Nick stiffen beneath her words.

"Nick?" She pulled slightly away. "Nick, what is it?"

"Kate, you don't understand." His voice was low and raspy and filled with an intense pain. It had lost the loving warmth of a moment ago. "Kate," he said slowly, "I'm not a father."

"What do you mean, Nick? Of course, you are. The papers . . . Elizabeth . . . Was it a mistake?" The fear took on a shape, a definition.

"No, that wasn't a mistake. It looks like I fathered the little girl biologically. It must have been right before Elizabeth walked out. But Kate, I . . . I'm not a father. I don't know the first thing about parenting."

"Of course not." Kate tried to smile, but the growing fear felt suffocating. "Nick, I'm sure every parent feels like that at first. And you haven't had even the usual nine months to adjust to Shelby's arrival. But—"

Her hands were moving as she spoke, as if the movement would make the words more understandable. Nick captured her fingers and held them still in her lap. "No, Kate, listen to me. You don't understand. I would be a horrible father. My own father nearly ruined my life and I won't do that to a child. I won't mess up her life. I'm no different, Kate. I've built a different kind of life for myself. This little girl wouldn't flourish in it, she'd fade. I . . . I can't do that, Kate. Look at me, you know me, you know what I'm about."

"I know—I thought I knew—that you were a kind, gentle, loving person. That's what makes a father, Nick."

"That's a romantic notion, Kate. Believe me, I know. Look at my life, even my business. Worldwide is opening four foreign offices next year. So where would that put a child of mine? Smack dab in the hands of hired help. What kind of life is that? That's the kind of life I had, Kate—a damnable one. I have to figure out what's best for her, not what society dictates. Don't you see? She's the one that matters here."

"Of course, she is. Nick, listen—"

"No, Kate, you listen. I would mess up that child's life. And I don't say this easily. Some men are cut out to be fathers and some aren't. That little girl needs a family."

But you could be a family, we could be a family, Kate cried out silently. But she couldn't say those words out aloud. When she spoke, her voice was controlled, the voice of a stranger. "But Nick," she said, "whether you think you'd make a good father or not isn't really a factor now. The fact is, you have a daughter."

Nick's face had tensed. He and Kate were no longer touching. A leaden weight pressed painfully against Kate's heart. She wanted to put her hands over her ears so she wouldn't hear what he said next, because she knew with an instinct born of the love she had for this man, that it would destroy something in her.

"Kate, listen to me. I'm not going to raise Shelby. It would be wrong for her. I can't, don't you see."

Kate froze. Her blood turned to ice.

"I've checked into a couple of things. My sister Sharon just got married. I talked to her this morning, and she'd like a baby. So maybe when she comes back in a couple of weeks—"

Kate's whole body was shaking now. "I can't believe what I'm hearing from you. This isn't a doll we're talking about. This is a child, your own flesh and blood."

Nick was silent.

"Nick, tell me this is some incredible joke. Tell me you don't mean this." The sting of tears pressed painfully against her lids. She didn't want to cry. She couldn't cry. She needed to be sane so that she could help Nick see that the man she loved more than life itself would not do this, would never consider such a thing.

"Kate," Nick said painfully, "this isn't easy for me."

Kate stared at him. She could see the pain in his eyes but she refused to acknowledge it. He meant what he was saying. He was truly going to do this horrible thing. "Nick, I can't believe this. I can't..." She shook her head.

Nick reached for her hand. "Kate, I thought you understood me. I've never lied to you. I've never pretended to be anything that I'm not. I'm doing what I think is best for the child."

"The child?" Kate's voice shrilled. "The child has a name. Shelby Bannister. That's her name. *Your* name." The tears began to fall now, and she brushed them away angrily with the back of her hand.

A great silence fell upon the room. A great hollow silence that was more frightening to Kate than any words they had spoken. This was not her Nick; this was not the man she loved. Slowly she rose from the couch and walked toward the door.

"Kate," Nick called after her. There was great pain in his voice.

Kate didn't look back. The tears fell unchecked now, running down her cheeks in wide rivers. And between the space of the den and the massive front door, she felt the tears wash over the splintered pieces of her heart.

Twelve

―――

"Kate, you need to sleep. The bags under your eyes could hold a week's worth of groceries." Harry sat on the threadbare couch in Kate's tiny living room a few days later and looked at her with concern. "And eat, honey. You need some food in you."

"I need to figure out how I can live without Nick, Harry," Kate whispered. Her voice was hoarse and tired. "You know, I really thought our love would make everything okay. I thought our life would come together somehow, that everything we both wanted in life would come true because we loved each other. I...I thought he'd change about some things, Harry...." She reached for another tissue.

"Maybe you didn't have the right to expect that, little one," Harry said gently.

Kate shook her head and the tears fell onto her sweatshirt. "Maybe not. Maybe I was fooling myself all along."

"But Nick never tried to fool you, Katherine. And what you have loved in that man is what he really is. Even if Shelby hadn't come along, you would have had to deal with that at some time or another."

"Maybe, Harry. I can't think anymore. I close my eyes and I think of her, of that lovely little girl. And I doze off and I dream of Nick, of loving him, of the joy he's filled me with and the completion he's brought to my life. And then I wake up and instead of everything coming together, it shatters into a thousand pieces."

"Maybe you should see Nick, talk to him."

Kate shook her head. "I can't. Nick has said it all. But I do have to see Shelby. I have to be sure she's okay." She looked up. "After all, she's a part of Nick."

She washed her face with ice-cold water to hide the effects of her tears, and bundled up in a warm wool jacket. Kate wasn't sure if the cold was outside her, or inside, but the jacket helped to comfort her a little. She called Sylvia to make sure Nick was at the office, then rushed over to the large white mansion across the park.

Carlton welcomed her warmly. There was concern about his eyes and when Kate asked about Shelby and Nick, he explained that Mr. Bannister did not look well. "Since you left the other day," he said, "Mr. Bannister has been keeping to himself. He checks on the little girl, but seems very preoccupied."

Kate nodded, held back the tears and headed for the guest room. On the way up the winding staircase, she made a decision. She couldn't control what Nick did, and she couldn't stop the pain inside her, but she could try to forget herself for a little while and provide Shelby with some security during these confusing days. And she'd do just that. She would not desert this baby. She'd love her, even if it were only for a few days or weeks. The resolution buoyed her spirits so that when she entered Shelby's room, she was smiling. Shelby reacted immediately, laughing and opening her arms for Kate to take her from the crib. Christina exited immediately and gratefully.

"Hi, sweetie," Kate said, and set to work changing a very damp diaper.

While Harry managed the company, Kate devoted herself to the newest Bannister in her life. The days spent with Shelby passed quickly, and by the end of a week, Shelby was calling for Kate when the doorbell rang early in the morning, and clung to her when she left at night. Kate always promised to come back, and she always did.

Kate never asked about Nick, but she soaked up the information Carlton subtly dropped. He told Kate that on Wednesday he had seen Nick going into Shelby's room. Another day he brought her a huge panda bear, which now sat at the foot of her bed. And on Thursday night, when Carlton did a last-minute house check before returning to his apartment over the garage, he had heard voices coming from the little girl's room. When he looked in, he saw Mr. Bannister putting the little girl back into her crib.

"She's a sweet little thing," Carlton said. "A charmer."

Kate smiled and tried to hold back the tears. A tiny flicker of hope almost worked its way into her heart, but Kate buried it. She couldn't think like that. Nick's sister was coming back soon, Carlton had said. She'd be here before Thanksgiving. And she had called once or twice to ask Nick questions about the baby.

"Carlton," Kate asked softly, "Does...does Mr. Bannister know I come over here each day?"

Carlton nodded. And then he smiled in that curious way he had and walked silently away.

"You're getting attached to her, little one," Harry said while he and Kate watched Shelby play on the floor of the office one day. "Is that wise?"

"She's a part of Nick," was all Kate could get out before the lump in her throat stopped the words. Then Harry piled them both in the car, because it was a slow day and one of the things Shelby loved most of all was riding through town in her tiny car seat in the back of the great white limo. She'd wave at people and clap her hands and giggle with delight as Kate sang, "Itsy bitsy spider," and walked her fingers up the little girl's legs.

Nick was aware of the outings; Kate knew Carlton kept him fully informed. She took his silence to mean approval, so she kept coming back to fill the little girl's days with love.

Once day Kate overstayed her time at the Bannister home and as she turned the handle of the door to leave, it opened from the other side. They stood face to face, just inches apart, Nick and Kate. Kate's heart twisted painfully, and all the love she had been busy burying beneath her care for Shelby soared to the surface.

Nick looked at her, his eyes as dark and lonely as the sea. In their depths Kate could see his overwhelming love for her.

"Oh, Kate," he said, and reached out to touch her. But Kate turned and fled before her heart broke right there on the cool marble floor. She ran down the brick sidewalk, all the way to her car, and drove to a shadowy corner of Loose Park where she parked the car and cried until she didn't think there were any tears left.

The weekend was long and painful without Shelby, but Kate knew Nick might be home and she couldn't see him again. She felt so weak, so encumbered by her love. Whereas before it had been her life force, her joy, the power inside her that made her days sing, now it held her chained in sadness and loneliness. At least when she was with Shelby she could forget for a while, could go beyond herself to the little girl who needed her.

On Sunday she drove by the house, just to feel close. The garage was open and Kate noticed Nick's car was gone. Carlton was out in the driveway, braving the freezing weather and polishing the town car that Nick rarely used.

Feeling safe, Kate drove in to say hello and give Shelby a hug.

"Where's my girl?" she asked brightly when Carlton walked over to her car. "I thought I'd say hello."

"Shelby's not here, Kate."

"She's not?" Fear tightened her voice, but then she noticed Carlton's smile and she relaxed. Although he wouldn't come near to admitting it, Carlton was already fond of Shelby. One day Kate had walked in on him giving the child a ride on his giant, black shoe while he held onto her hands to keep her from falling off.

Carlton looked at his watch. "They'll be back for dinner. Went out yesterday, too."

They will be back. Kate pondered the words. She was the only one who took Shelby out of the house. Christina didn't drive and Carlton was here. But Nick was gone.

Kate bit back the questions that jumped to her lips. It wasn't her business. She had no right to ask. Instead she said, "Looks like you're working hard, Carlton. The car looks beautiful."

Carlton stood back and looked at his handiwork. "Well, good. Miss Sharon isn't always an easy person to please."

"Sharon?"

"Mr. Bannister's sister. It appears she and her husband—the most recent one—are arriving earlier than expected. They will be here tomorrow, and this is the car she likes me to use when I drive her around."

"I see." Kate stared at the car. She could see her distorted reflection in it, but the fear and pain in her eyes were not distorted. They were very real.

"Will you be coming by tomorrow, Kate?" Carlton asked.

"I, ah, I don't know, Carlton. I'll call you."

She rolled the window back up and drove out of the driveway quickly. She didn't want Carlton to see the tears. He wouldn't understand; she couldn't even explain them to herself. But the feeling that she was losing yet another person she loved stayed with her through the long and lonely night.

With great resolve, Kate kept herself from calling Carlton the next day. Weaning, maybe that was what she needed. And maybe Sharon Bannister whatever-her-new-last-name-was might be a lovely, warm person who would be a perfect mother to Shelby. Maybe things would work out for the Bannisters. But none of those thoughts filled the cold, horrible, hollow feeling that consumed her.

"Hey, Katy," Harry said the next morning when Kate walked into the office, "get on that phone. Nick wants to talk to you. He's called twice already today and left a message yesterday after you left."

Kate's heart stopped. "Did he say why he was calling?"

"Wants to talk to you."

"About Shelby?"

Harry shrugged. "I asked, and he said the tyke is doing fine but that she missed you. If you ask me I think he wants to talk about you and him."

Kate shook her head. "There isn't anything to talk about." And she filled the day with errands and meetings and staying out of the office, so she didn't have to feel the pain each of the next eight times Nick called to talk to her.

A quick call to Carlton when she stopped for lunch assured her Shelby was doing fine. "But she asks for you, Kate. You need to come and see her. How about tomorrow?" And then he added with quiet understanding. "Miss Sharon and that man she brought home will be out for the day shopping."

"And Nick?"

"He'll be at the office," Carlton said.

"Okay, it's a date, Carlton. Tell Shelby I'm coming. Tell her...tell her I love her."

She picked up Shelby the next day in a shiny, just-washed White Knight, Shelby's favorite car because she could play with the remote control on the television set. "I think we'll do the town, Carlton," Kate said. "Lunch at Crown Center, a visit to the toy store, a ride on the escalator and maybe we'll take in a pet store or two."

Shelby waved happily to Carlton and Kate tucked her happily into her car seat in the back of the limo.

"Ap' juice?" she asked Kate, and Kate hugged her tightly and filled a small cup with apple juice from the car refrigerator. They drove through the Plaza and toward Crown Center, Shelby thrilling Kate with cheerful monosyllabic labels for everything they passed by.

"But, Harry, I have to talk to her," Nick insisted. He stood in front of Harry's desk in the limo office, his hands jammed in the pockets of his suit pants.

"She's not here, Nick. Honest. And it's a good thing because you sure look like hell."

Nick gave a short, pained laugh, then he took in a lungful of air. "I love her, you know. Kate's my life."

"It's complicated."

"Yeah, tell me about it. But the one thing that isn't is how I feel about her. And she needs to give me a chance. I'm working on it all, Harry, I am."

Harry offered him a smile and a doughnut.

"Life's crazy, Harry," Nick said, picking up the pastry.

"You could say that."

"You never stop learning, do you?"

"Me?"

"You, me, everyone."

"Nope, Nick, and that's the good thing about it all."

Nick smiled. There had to still be a chance. He'd hurt Kate terribly, but there was a way to work this out.

Things somehow felt lighter now. Maybe it was just being in her office, smelling the traces of that light perfume she wore. Sometimes he could smell it on Shelby after Kate had been there. The thought of Shelby deepened the smile. Damn. You live and learn. He checked his watch. Okay, he'd track Kate down later. In the meantime he'd go see Shelby. Take her for a ride in that car seat she loved so much. Forget business for a day.

"'Loons," Shelby crooned as they drove down Westport Road and passed a portrait artist on the corner sketching a subject. The young man had tied a bouquet of colorful balloons to his easel to attract attention.

"Right, Shelby," Kate said. "Balloons. Want one?"

"'Loons!'' Shelby said, clapping her hands together.

Kate pulled up to the curb across the street and looked at Shelby. "I'll be back in a jiffy, sweetie, and I'll bring a big red balloon with me."

After grabbing a coin purse from her bag, she darted through the traffic, offered the man a bill for the balloon and headed back toward the car. A blaring horn forced her back a step while a speeding driver whizzed by, and then Kate, still clutching the balloon, headed back.

It all happened in an instant but Kate would replay it for hours, that split second before she reached the car. That earth-shaking, terrifying second, when a young kid sauntering down the street spotted the keys, the open door and what looked like an empty limo. That one, irrevocable, heart-stopping second when the stranger jumped into the car.

Thirteen

He was tall and gangly and had scanned the street for a fraction of a second to see if he could spot a chauffeur. Then, without further thought, he had jumped into the car, slammed the door and took off down the street.

Kate's whole body filled with fear. She didn't look right or left. Her mind a white screen of rage, she saw nothing but the flash of her car traveling down the crowded street.

She took off after it the instant it moved, screaming out for him to stop, pleading for Shelby's safety, and running faster than her legs had ever moved before. Her mind was numb and her body propelled by fury.

Blind to anything but protecting Shelby, Kate caught the handle of the door and with the car still moving, jerked it open.

A pale, frightened youth slammed on the brakes.

Kate reached over and put the car in park. Then she grabbed the kid by the shoulders, pulling him, dragging him out of the car. Her heart beat furiously and she was only vaguely aware of the tears that streamed down her face. "You fool," she cried and pushed him flat against the car.

Behind him, through the tinted glass of the window, Shelby's huge blue eyes looked out at her.

A policeman pried Kate away from the youth, took him by the arm and led him over to the side, away from the gathering crowd. Almost immediately, from behind her, arms wrapped her gently against a hard, rapidly breathing chest. Shelby grinned. "Da-da?" she said.

And the man on whom Shelby's eyes were focused slowly turned Kate around in his arms.

"Oh, my darling, Kate," was all he said.

"Nick . . . I . . . what—" Kate couldn't hear her own voice over the rapid breathing of her heart.

Still holding her in the warmth of his arms, Nick opened the back door and with the help of a passerby, lifted Shelby from the car seat. He hugged them both tightly to his chest. "If either of you'd been hurt, I . . ." His voice was filled with agony. Kate looked up into his face. She couldn't think, couldn't put everything together: Nick, her fear, Shelby's face as the car moved away from her, her body's exhaustion. It was all too much. She felt her knees begin to buckle just as the policeman walked back to where they stood.

"Mr. Bannister, why don't you take them home. I'll take care of the limo and be in touch with you later."

After thanking him, Nick took Kate and Shelby back to his car, which he had left in the middle of the street, the engine still running. A dozen cars waited impatiently behind it.

In minutes they were blocks away, and Nick pulled over to the curb in a quiet, tree-lined neighborhood. He held Kate to him, winding his fingers in her hair and kissing away her tears.

Shelby sat in her car seat, happy and delighted with a bottle of apple juice clutched tightly in her hands.

"Nick," Kate began, but her voice broke and instead of talking, she buried her head in his chest.

"I was looking for you, sweetheart. Carlton told me where you were headed." He tipped her head up so she was looking at him. "Kate, I love you. I love you more than you'll ever begin to know. And when I saw you and Shelby in danger like that, I knew that if anything happened to you both, I would die, too, because there wouldn't be anything left."

"Shelby—"

"Shelby's like you Kate, persistent. She's done something to me. Once you started taking her out for rides in the car, it was the one thing that would make her happy. So when I was home, I'd take her out, to stop her crying and to keep Christina from quitting. And we started to get to know each other when we were out in the car like that, driving around. I didn't quite realize what she was doing to me until Sharon came home."

"Sharon?" Kate cringed instinctively. In her mind, this woman she had never met had become a foe. It was irrational, she knew, but very real.

"Yeah, my sister and her latest husband got in after midnight one night. And Sharon rushed up to Shelby's room and picked her right up out of her bed. I froze, Kate. There was no way in hell I was going to let her have my daughter."

His voice broke and he took a slow, stabilizing breath. "My daughter," he said again, more slowly, tasting the words as if for the first time.

Beside him, Kate's whole body shook with emotion.

Nick went on. "I haven't worked everything out. There are a lot of things we need to talk about, Kate. But Shelby doesn't seem to care much whether everything is worked out. I know I've hurt you, Kate. I know you've seen things in me you couldn't possibly love—"

Kate reached up and touched his cheek. "Nick," she said softly, "I love you. I never stopped loving you. I never will."

"Well, then," Nick said, and then he coughed to cover the catch in his voice. "Well, then," he said again starting up the car, "in that case, Shelby and I have something to show you." He turned and winked at the little girl in the backseat.

"Nick, you don't need to show me anything. I just want to hold you, to be with you and Shelby, that's all."

"Shh," Nick said, stopping her words with the press of fingers against his lips. "Don't ruin our surprise."

He headed south, crossing over the state line, and in a short time they were on the edge of the city where houses fell back from the roads and rolling fields separated newly built neighborhoods from one another.

Soft music and Shelby's chatter filled the car, and love filled everything else as Kate felt her life swelling, taking in everything around her.

Finally Nick turned off the paved main road and drove over a hill, past lovely converted farmhouses and some newer homes built to fit into the natural landscape. He slowed down, nearly stopped, and turned into a drive that was bordered by a freshly painted fence. The road curved up to a large two-story white house that sprawled out across treed acres.

Kate froze. Had she misunderstood? Had he found a different home for Shelby? She couldn't breathe, couldn't speak.

"Well?" Nick said beside her, "what do you think? There's a pond in the back and plenty of room for a pool, as well. Sometimes they saw deer in the mornings from the porch."

"They?" Kate croaked.

"The people who lived here."

"Lived here?"

Nick looked back at Shelby. "She's slow, princess, but she'll catch on. It's probably because of the shutters."

He looked back at Kate. "I'm sorry about that. I tried to get them to paint the shutters green, but we couldn't find anyone to do it the week before Thanksgiving."

"Shutters?"

Nick held her head between his hands, ignoring the tears streaming down her cheeks. "Sometimes Shelby makes better sentences than you do."

"Oh, Nick," she breathed.

"I'm only doing what the policeman ordered, Kate." He opened the door of the car and lifted Shelby out of her car seat. Kate stood at his side, her eyes slowly moving back and forth between the beautiful home and Nick and Shelby.

"The officer of the law said to take you both home, Kate," Nick said softly.

"Home," Shelby said, and reached out to touch Kate's hair.

"Home," Kate said in a hushed voice.

"Will you marry us?" Nick asked then. "It's kind of a part of the deal."

Kate took Shelby into her arms. And then she pressed herself into the full circle of Nick's embrace, certain that in just a minute she would burst. "Will I marry you?" she murmured. "Oh, Nick..."

"I think, Shelby," Nick said to his daughter, "that she means yes. Her vocabulary needs a little work today." He swung the little girl down to her feet, keeping hold of one hand while Kate held tightly to the other.

Kate looked into Nick's eyes, down into the depths of his soul. "Nick Bannister, it means try and stop me," Kate whispered. "It means forever, it means, my love—"

"Sometimes, Kate Morelli, you talk too much," Nick said, and while Shelby Bannister wiggled her tiny body between their legs, Nick stopped Kate's talk with his lips, showing Kate a far nicer way than words to seal forever.

*   *   *   *   *

COMING NEXT MONTH FROM

Silhouette

Sensation
romance with a special mix of suspense, glamour and drama

A TALENT FOR LOVE Saranne Dawson
BELOVED DREAMER Anne Henry
A PERILOUS EDEN Heather Graham Pozzessere
FLIRTING WITH DANGER Linda Turner

Special Edition
longer, satisfying romances with mature heroines and lots of emotion

THE LAST GOOD MAN ALIVE Myrna Temte
ONE LOST WINTER Diana Whitney
AGAINST ALL ODDS Joleen Daniels
DOUBLE DARE Christine Rimmer
SHADOWS ON THE SAND Maggi Charles
SWEET LIES, SATIN SIGHS Bay Matthews

COMING NEXT MONTH

GLORY, GLORY
Linda Lael Miller

Glory Parsons had been made to flee her
hometown — and leave behind the man who'd
stolen her heart. He'd never discovered the
heartbreaking price she'd paid. He didn't know that
his adopted niece was really his child …

LOOKING FOR TROUBLE
Nancy Martin

Sheila Malone was a good cop and the last thing she
needed was a rich smart-mouthed man getting in
her way. Especially when the man in question was
drop-dead gorgeous and the key to a five-year-old
murder.

THE BRIDAL PRICE
Barbara Boswell

Carling Templeton was an enlightened twentieth-
century woman — about to be sold into marriage
like some sort of chattel. Arrogant, insufferable
rancher Kane McClellan needed to be taught a
lesson. How could he have put a price on love?

COMING NEXT MONTH

UPON A MIDNIGHT CLEAR
Laura Leone

Bah humbug! That's how Fiona Larkin felt at Christmastime when everyone else spent the holidays with their families. Even security consultant Eli Becker wanted to go home rather than find out who was breaking into Oak Hill Pet Motel. What could they be after?

THE PENDRAGON VIRUS
Cait London

Sam Loring had a ruthless and very masculine lack of concern for the domestic problems of his staff. So when Dallas Pendragon bet him that he wouldn't last a month as a working mother, he expected to win ... and the stakes were high!

HANDSOME DEVIL
Joan Hohl

Selena McInnes was undaunted and unimpressed by strong men, until she met May's *Man of the Month*, handsome devil Luke Branson, in this passionate sequel to *The Gentleman Insists*.

Life and death drama in this gripping new novel of passion and suspense

Following a vicious attack on a tough property developer and his beautiful wife, eminent surgeon David Compton fought fiercely to save both lives, little knowing just how deeply he would become involved in a complex web of deadly revenge. Ginette Irving, the cool and practical theatre sister, was an enigma to David, but could he risk an affair with the worrying threat to his career and now the sinister attempts on his life?

W●RLDWIDE

Price: £3.99   Published: May 1991

Available from Boots, Martins, John Menzies, W.H. Smith, Woolworths and other paperback stockists.

Also available from Mills and Boon Reader Service, P.O. Box 236, Thornton Road, Croydon, Surrey CR9 3RU

Four Silhouette Desires absolutely free!

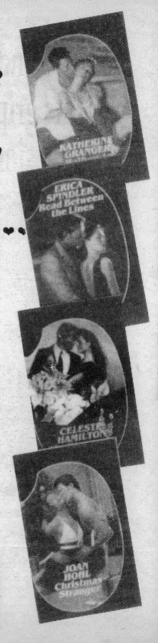

Provocative, highly sensual love stories designed for the sophisticated reader. The enticing plots provide a distinctive mix of exciting romantic encounters and unpredictable reactions.

Now you can enjoy four Silhouette Desire romances as a free gift from Silhouette plus the chance to have more delivered to your door every single month.

Turn the page for details of how to apply, and claim 2 extra free gifts!

An irresistible offer from Silhouette

Here's a personal invitation from Silhouette to become a regular reader of Desire: and to welcome you we'd like you to have four books, a cuddly teddy bear and a special Mystery Gift - absolutely free and without obligation.

Then, each month you could look forward to receiving 6 more Silhouette Desires delivered direct to your door for just £1.50 each, post and packing free. Plus our newsletter featuring author news, competitions, special offers and lots more.

This invitation comes with no strings attached. You can cancel or suspend your subscription at any time and still keep your free books and gifts.

Its so easy. Send no money now. Simply fill in the coupon below at once and post to: Silhouette Reader Service, FREEPOST, PO Box 236, Croydon, Surrey CR9 9EL.

- - - - - NO STAMP REQUIRED - - - - →

YES! Please rush me my 4 Free Silhouette Desires and 2 Free Gifts! Please also reserve me a Reader Service Subscription. If I decide to subscribe I can look forward to receiving 6 brand new Silhouette Desires each month for just £9.00, delivered direct to my door. If I choose not to subscribe I shall write to you within 10 days - but I am free to keep the books and gifts. I can cancel or suspend my subscription at any time. I am over 18. Please write in BLOCK CAPITALS.

Mrs/Miss/Ms/Mr _____   EP11SD

Address _____

_____

_____ Postcode _____
(Please don't forget to include your postcode)

Signature _____

The right is reserved to refuse an application and change the terms of this offer. Offer expires December 31st 1991. Readers in Southern Africa please write to P.O. Box 2125, Randburg, South Africa. Other Overseas and Eire, send for details. You may be mailed with other offers from Mills & Boon and other reputable companies as a result of this application. If you would prefer not to share in this opportunity, please tick box. ☐